Urban Welsh

Urban Welsh

New Short Fiction

Edited by

Lewis Davies

PARTHIAN

Parthian
The Old Surgery
Napier Street
Cardigan
SA43 1ED

www.parthianbooks.co.uk

First published in 2005
© The Authors 2005
This collection © Parthian 2005
All Rights Reserved

ISBN 1-902638-42-5

Editor: Lewis Davies

Cover design by Marc Jennings
Printed and bound by Dinefwr Press, Llandybïe, Wales
Typeset by type@lloydrobson.com and Parthian

Parthian is an independent publisher which works with
the support of the Arts Council of Wales and the Welsh
Books Council

British Library Cataloguing in Publication Data – A
cataloguing record for this book is available from the
British Library

Stories

I've written a number of stories about Michigan country – the country is always true – what happens in the stories is fiction.
Ernest Hemingway

Fresh Apples

Rachel Trezise

When you get oil from a locomotive engine all over your best blue jeans, it looks like shit, black and sticky. I can see it's black, even in the dark. I stand on the sty and try to brush it away with the back of my hand, bent awkward over the fence, but it sticks to my skin, and then there's nowhere to wipe my hands. Laugh they would, Rhys Davies and Kristian if they could see me now. Don't know why I wore my best stuff. 'Wear clean knickers,' my mother'd say, 'in case you have an accident.' She'd say knickers even when she meant pants. She's a feminist, see. But it's not like anyone would notice if I was wearing pants or not. Johnny Mental from up the street, he said when he was at school the police would pay him at the end of the day to look for bits of fingers and bits of intestines here, before he went home for tea. If it can do that, if it can slice your tubes like green beans, who's going to notice if you had skid marks in your kecks? I can still hear the train chugging away, or perhaps it's my imagination. Over in the town I can hear drunk people singing but closer I can hear cicadas – that noise you think only exists in American films to show you that something horrific is about to happen – it's real. It's hot too. Even in the night it's still hot and I'm panting like a dog. I'm sure it's this weather that's making me fucking crazy. I'm alive anyway; I can feel my blood pumping so it's all been a waste of time. Forget it now, that's the thing to do. Oh, you want to know about it, of course you do. Nosy bastard you are. Well I'll tell you and then I'll forget it, and you can forget it too. And just remember this: I'm not proud of it. Let's get that straight from the outset. The whole thing is a bloody encumbrance. (New word that, encumbrance. I found it in my father's things this morning.)

Thursday night it started, but the summer has been going on forever, for years it seems like, the sun visors down on the café's and fruiterer's in town, the smell of barbecued food wafting on the air, and never going away. And the smell of mountain fires, of timber crumbling and being swallowed by a rolling wave of orange flame. On the Bwlch we were, at the entrance to the forestry. There used to be a climbing frame and a set of swings made from the logs from the trees. It's gone now but we still go there, us and the car and van shaggers. Sitting on a picnic table with my legs hanging over the edge so I could see down Holly's top when she leaned forward on the bench, her coffee colour skin going into two perfect, hard spheres, like snooker balls, or drawer knobs, poking the cartoon on her T-shirt out at either side. She was drinking blackcurrant, the plastic bottle to her mouth, the purple liquid inside it swishing back and fore. I asked her for some. I wouldn't normally – I'm shy, I'd lose my tongue, but my mouth was dry and scratchy from the sun. Yes, she said, but when I gave the bottle back she wiped the rim on the hem of her skirt like I had AIDS. Kristian and Rhys Davies John Davies, they had handfuls of stone chippings, throwing them at Escorts when they went passed, their techno music jumping. Jealous they are, of the cars and stereos but fuck that dance music, it's Metallica for me. (Don't tell them that.) It's his real name by the way, Rhys Davies John Davies, the first part after some gay Welsh poet, the second after his armed robber father, shacked up in Swansea Prison.

Every time something passed us, a lorry or a motorbike, it grated on the cattle grid in the road. That's how Kristian came up with the cow tipping idea. Only we couldn't go cow tipping because you can only tip cows when they're sleeping, in the middle of the night and it'd take ten of us to move one, so Holly had to go one better.

'Let's go and start a fire!' she said.

'Don't be stupid,' I said. 'We should be proud of this mountain Hol. They haven't got mountains like this in England. And you'll kill all the nature.'

'Nature?!' she said. She rolled her eyes at Jaime and Angharad. 'It's not the fuckin' Amazonian rain forest, Matt.' She can be a cow when she wants, see. 'C'mon girls,' she said, and she flicked her curly hair out of her face. 'When there's a fire, what else is there?'

'A fire engine?' Jaime said.

'Exactly. Firemen. Proper men!' And she started up off into the trees, shaking her tiny denim arse at us. The girls followed her and then the boys followed the girls. So that just left me. And Sarah.

Sarah, Jaime's cerebral palsy kid sister. She's not abnormal or ugly, just a little bit fat, and she rocks back and fore slightly, and she has a spasm in her hand that makes her look like she's doing something sexual to herself all the time. But she's brighter than Jaime gives her credit for, even when she's got that big, green chewing gum bubble coming out of her mouth and hiding her whole face. I just never knew what to say to her – how to start a conversation. I smiled at her clumsily and tried to giggle at the silence. We stayed like that, her sitting on her hands, chewing her gum loudly so I could hear her saliva swish around in her mouth, until a fireman came with thick, black stubble over his face, fanning the burning ferns out with a giant fly squat because he couldn't get his engine up onto the mountain.

'Come and get us you sexy fucker,' Holly was shouting at him, hiding her face behind a tree. That's when I went home.

On Friday morning, on the portable tv in the kitchen there was an appeal from Rhymney Valley Fire Service for kids to stop setting fire to the mountains.

'Nine times out of ten it's arson,' the man's voice boomed. 'It's children with matches.' The volume's broke, see, it either has to be on full, or it has to be on mute.

'That's kids is it?' My mother said, hanging over the draining board, a red gingham cloth stuffed into a tall, transparent cylinder. 'I always thought it was bits of glass left in the ground starting it. It can happen like that when it's hot can't it?' My father ignored her, standing at arms length from the frying pan, turning sausages over with his chef's tongs. She gave up pushing the cloth down into the glass and washed the bubbles out under the cold tap. I watched the rest of the announcement spooning Coco Pops into my mouth, the milk around them yellowy and sweet.

'The mountains are tinder dry,' the man said, 'so please don't go near them with matches. While we're attending to an arson attack there could be a serious house fire in the town.' I remembered the look of helplessness on the fireman's face while he sweated over the ferns, Holly asking him to fuck her. He knew that as soon as he'd gone we'd start it again so he'd have to come back, sweating again. I opened one of the blue cover English exercise books my father was marking at the kitchen table before he got up to cook breakfast, and read some kid's modern version of Hamlet. Crap it was, but I found two new words, psychodrama and necromancy.

Later, at Rhys Davies' house, his mother was still cleaning spew off plastic beer-garden tables, and his father was still in jail, so Kristian and Rhys, they were drinking a box of cheap red wine.

'Matt,' Kristian said, dropping the playstation pad on the carpet. 'Holly got her tits out last night.'

'No she fuckin' didn't,' I said.

'She fuckin' did and you missed it,' he said.

'No she didn't,' Rhys said.

They offered me the wine but I didn't want it. I went to the kitchen and scoured it for Mrs Davies' chocolate. She had a shit load hidden from Rhys' sister in Mr Davies' old lunch box, under the basket weave cutlery tray.

'I wouldn't poke 'er anyway,' Kristian was saying when I went back. 'She's a snobby bitch. She's the only form five I haven't poked and I don't want to poke 'er. She's frigid inshee?'

I didn't know what frigid meant but I made a note in my head to find out and another one to remember to poke some girl before people started to think I was gay.

'Imagine all the new girls when we start tech!' Kristian said. We were starting tech in a month. Kristian wanted to be a plumber. His father told him, with some prison guard standing nearby, that he'd always have money if he was a plumber. Strange, because Mr Davies was a plumber but he tried to rob an all night garage with a stick in a black bag. Kristian and me, we were doing a bricklaying NVQ because the careers teacher said it was a good course.

'The girls from the church school'll be starting the same time and none of them've got pinhole pussies,' Kristian said. 'Johnny Mental told me, they're all slags.'

I was leaning out of the window watching the elderly woman next door feeding lettuce to her tortoise. It was still really hot but she was wearing a cream colour Aran cardigan. I was wondering if there was a job somewhere which involved collecting words to put into a dictionary or something, or a course which taught you to play drums like Tommy Lee so I could throw sticks into the air after a roll and catch them in my teeth because I didn't find bricks and girls with big fannies that exciting. I unwrapped the chocolate but it had already melted.

That night we were on the mountain again, standing on the roof of the old brick caretaker's hut looking down into the town at the small groups of women walking like matchstick people into pubs in their sunburn, their too tight trousers and gold strap sandals, the men in blue jeans and ironed shirts. Holly, Angharad and Jaime, they came up via the new road because they had Holly's Collie dog on a lead. There's a farm across the road, see, with a sheepdog in the field, a white one with black patches around its eyes like a canine panda. It barks at the sight of another dog and keeps barking until the farmer comes over and tells us to fuck off before he shoots us. He thinks anyone under the age of eighteen is committing some heinous crime just by breathing. So we missed looking down into Holly's cheesecloth blouse as she passed underneath us. Sarah was five minutes behind them, wobbling over the banking, her thick white shins shining, her short yellow hair bouncing on her fat, pink head. There was some kind of in joke going on with Kristian and Rhys and Angharad and Holly and Jaime. They all seemed to be winking at one another, or talking to one another but with no words coming out of their mouths. I thought I caught Kristian doing a wanker signal behind my back but I passed it off as a hallucination with the sun being so fucking hot. Then the dog began to cough.

'Holly, there's something wrong with your dog,' I said. 'I think it's dying.'

'Take her to the dam,' Holly said, because she thinks I'm some kind of PA, put on the planet to look after her. I took the dog to the dam, watched it lap up the slimy water and when I came back everyone had gone. You get used to that when you're a teacher's son, your friends disappearing to smoke fags or sniff glue and aerosol canisters without you.

It had been an hour before I thought of something to say to her and even then I didn't say anything. She blew a great big bubble; I saw it growing from the corner of my eye where I was sitting next to her on the grass. I put my finger straight up to her face and burst it. For a second everything smelt like fresh apples. That's what made me want to kiss her. I just pinned her to the ground and kissed her, my eyes wide open, her tiny blue eyes smiling up at me. Inside her mouth the chewing gum tasted more like cider. I found her tits under a thick vest but there was no shape to them. Her whole chest was like an old continental quilt, all soft and lumpy under its duvet cover. I kept on kissing her, my front teeth bashing against hers. She didn't flex a muscle, just lied there looking amused by me. When I had her bush in my hand, her pubes rough and scratchy, that's when I noticed the dog looking at me funny, its brown eyes staring down its long snout. I tidied Sarah's clothes up the best I could and ran away sniffing my fingers and I thought that was the end of it.

On Saturday morning – the next day – Kristian, Rhys Davies and me, we were sitting on the pavement in the street flipping two and five pence coins. It's the main thoroughfare, see, for the town. When it's sunny we just sit there watching women going shopping in cotton dresses, pushing prams with big, bald babies inside. Our street was built during the coal boom, my father said, a terrace with a row of small houses for the miners and their families on our side, and a row of bigger ones with front gardens opposite for the mine managers and supervisors. Johnny Mental was sitting on his porch wearing sunglasses, drinking lager, his teeth orange and wonky. Someone was painting their front door a few yards away with a portable radio playing soul music, Diana Ross or some shit. A big burgundy Vauxhall Cavalier came around the corner, real slow like an old man on a hill, until it stopped next to us and I saw Jaime in the back looking worried, her eyes tiny and sinking back into her head. Her father got out, a tall, broad man who looked like Tom Baker in Doctor Who, and he picked Kristian up by the collar of his best Kangol T-shirt because that's who he was closest to.

'You raped my daughter you little prick,' he said. My stomach did a somersault inside me and got all twisted up. I looked at Jaime through the smoked glass of the car but she had the back of her head to me, looking at Johnny Mental. He'd stood up and was watching us; the lager can tilted in mid air towards his chin. Jaime's father punched Kristian in the midriff, cleverly so that none of us could see it, but we all knew it. 'Look at you – you dirty fuckin' paedophile,' he said to Rhys Davies and he spat on the pavement next to his feet. 'Won't be long until you're eating breakfast with your father, will it?' he said, but he didn't touch him. He picked me up by my ears, by my ears. My heart stopped beating then and my blood drained away.

I don't know where it went but I felt it go. 'Was it you?' he said, and he knocked the back of my head against the brick wall of the house. 'Did you rape my daughter, you sick little cunt?' I could feel myself disappearing in his grasp when I heard Jaime shouting. 'C'mon. C'mon Dad, get in the car.' I heard the door slam behind him but it didn't sound anything like relief.

'You've gone all fuckin' white,' Rhys said, looking down at me when the burgundy car had been out of the street for a good two minutes.

'So have you,' I said, even though I couldn't see him properly. All I could really see was the bright yellow light of the sun but I imagined Johnny Mental smirking at me from across the road. I was thinking that if a stick in a bag was actually armed robbery then just having a cock could make a kiss and a crap fumble into a rape. I tried to look as confused as Kristian and Rhys were, as we all looked at each other, pale skinned and speechless, and I tried to drift back to myself.

I never really got there. My parents went to the town hall that night to watch a play about an old writer dying of the consumption. I went walking. I walked through the comprehensive school, even though I thought I'd done that for the last time after my exams three months ago. I didn't have the energy to lift my feet but at the same time they seemed to lift all by themselves. Over the running track I kept thinking about Sarah. I tried not to. I tried to think about words but the only ones which came were the ones that came out of Tom Baker's mouth with a spray of bitter saliva, sick and paedophile and rape. And underneath them

I could see Sarah on the grass, smiling at me, her skirt hitched up her fat legs. There was no way it was rape, or even molestation, she was fucking smiling at me, and she's fourteen, not a child. I'm not a paedophile. Jaime's sixteen and she's sucked the whole village's dick; that's what I told myself. But the longer I looked at the picture the more her smile turned into a frown, like looking at the Mona Lisa too long, and she was starting to shake, her arms flailing on the ends of her wrists. Then I was here, on the railway track, lying down, the rails cutting into my hamstrings and the small of my back. I wasn't sure if I wanted to die. No, I didn't want to die. Not forever anyway, only until it was over, until it was all forgotten. I remembered Geography classes in school, where the teacher would talk about physics instead because he was a physics teacher really and we'd get bored and stare down here to the track and talk about how many people had died here. Kristian said there was a woman who tied herself in a black bag and rolled onto the track so that when the train came she wouldn't be able to get up and run. I didn't need to do that. I stayed perfectly still. Didn't even slap the gnats biting my face. When the train came the clackety-clack rhythm it made froze me to the spot. I just closed my eyes. When I opened them again the train had gone, gone right past me on the opposite track and splashed my legs with black oil. I don't know if I'm brave or just stupid. It isn't easy to be sixteen, see, and it isn't that easy to die.

Uncle Mehdï's Carpet Deal

Rhian Saadat

Our Auntie Gwen loved all things exotic, and until she married (and she married late), she would clutter Gran's front room with souvenirs from her travels – postcards she had sent to herself and Gran; black-and-gold plastic gondolas from Venice, moored forever either side of the mantelpiece; costume dolls from the Black Forest; one large, carved cuckoo clock from Lucerne, and any number of velveteen bulls from Spain. It was as if something was missing from the core of her life, and she was trying her best to fill herself with the knowledge of other places. Not being that well-educated, she mistook the cheap trappings of tourism for a little bit of belonging. You couldn't really blame her, except that she was getting on, still travelling, but without the arrival bit.

And then, she disappeared off to Paris one weekend,

never saying a word, and returned, married to a man we had never had a hint of. We thought it strange, since she usually returned from Paris with Eiffel towers dangling on the end of key rings, but this time there was a good-looking man dangled on her arm. Someone she had met on her travels, she had smiled, someone she loved. I didn't mention him before because he is a foreigner – a Political Refugee. He seemed polite, warm even, but Gran put her foot down then. Said she wouldn't have him, whoever he was, messing up the house. He's called Abbas – Gwen did her best to break the ice – after a king. But Gran wasn't listening; she was the only royal member of our family. And that's when Gwen and her latest souvenir, her PA, as she referred to him playfully, decided to return to France, leaving Gran's place looking pretty bare for a palace, pruned back to its lace curtains and fireside chairs.

Sometime later, our new Uncle Ab revealed to Gwen the true extent of his lineage – a family of enormous proportions: carpet merchants – and every single one of them eager to visit them to share their newly found happiness. Gwen surrounded herself with the plastic boats, threatened to row away. It's a cultural thing, her husband pleaded. So's mine, Gwen had replied, defiantly.

And the relatives came from all around the world, and Gwen was polite – happy, even – and made an effort to learn Farsi, and to cook rice so that each grain of it stood to attention, huddled in the pan. It beat packet rice any day, and she became something of an expert in Middle Eastern Food. She was good like that, Auntie Gwen. Like a bloody sponge, Gran had said, and it was true – she soaked up Abbas's culture like she was born to it; like it was the thing she had been looking for most of her life. And then, Uncle Ab's older brother Mehdi paid them a visit.

Uncle Mehdi was, in fact, the king of Persia; I'm writing metaphorically, of course, because it might help to establish a perspective. And, after all – who says royalty cannot be created by a name, a state of mind, or even be defined by the robust health of a bank account? Not that he had a bank account, you must understand; this was before the arrival of pin-striped managers and accountants, and his money was – reputedly – sewn into fat and lumpy mattresses, piled high amongst the other treasures in his houses scattered about the towns and mountains of old Iran.

And this greatly respected uncle was the kind of man who, even as he approached his seventieth birthday by Gregorian calculations, had so much get up and go he could never be found, until he decided, one day, to go and see his brother and Gwen in their modest pavilion in the Western suburbs beyond Paris. With Mehdi, there was always a reason for everything he decided to do. He never spent time travelling unless it held the possibility of great profit. His long-awaited arrival was conducted on the scale of a state visit – or a military campaign, even – clouds of diesel fumes farting a path towards destination, punctuating the arrival, as if by magic, of a cortege of Hummer-sized taxis driven by drivers as roadweary as if they had just driven all the way from Tehran via Turkey and Afghanistan. The doors of the vehicles burst open; the contents – suitcases, assorted relatives, and enough dried fruit and saffron strands to keep the army going for months, if necessary – tumbled into the street in bountiful heaps, much to the annoyance of Auntie Gwen's neighbours. It wasn't the mess and the commotion, she would tell us later, so much as the squeaking garden gate, which – from the moment of Uncle Mehdi's arrival – protested, from morning to night as people slipped in and out, nipping into the village for fresh bread, for black cherry jam, for Marseille soap and eau-de-cologne. That Mehdi, said Auntie Gwen, not even attempting to conceal her skewed admiration, was the kind of man who lived and breathed, not just his own perfumed skin, but the aromas of the world's most precious antiquities: ancient books; Moorish astrolabes; Phoenician glass vessels – sand still clinging to their undulating rims – jewelled drinking cups; gold plates, and large carved doors that opened into nowhere lands. His beds and sofas were patchworks of carpets and festooned silks, which left the sleepers dreaming of journeys amongst clouds and migrating cranes, waking with a new sense of adventure, and dust in their hair. Unnatural, said Auntie Gwen, yet beautiful. We could tell, then, that Gwen had moved on from plastic bulls. She'd stopped travelling, in fact, and had arrived. Gran stopped talking to her around this time, said she'd grown too fanciful, that Gwen's head was being stuffed up with dirty thoughts. But it wasn't; she didn't like all the fuss and the visits, it's true, because they interfered with her gardening routine, but there were things she grew to appreciate: Uncle Mehdi knew things, and what he didn't know about bits and bobs wasn't worth knowing. He advised Auntie Gwen to part with her knick-knacks from her early Grand Tour, especially the cuckoo clock – in fact he was rather rude about the clock – and instead to accompany them to the auction houses in Paris: invest her small savings in real works of art. Such notions were hard to ignore in the presence of someone so successful, so rich. Every last fibre of his home in Tehran, she said, came with a label – a price with zeros winding towards the horizon, written from left to right in his battered leather-bound book. Even the clothes he wore – and Auntie Gwen would point them out to us in the photographs – his Prada shoes, his trendy Gucci jeans, his Versace shirts – even the shirt off his back would be sold to the right buyer for the right price. But Uncle Mehdi's real prowess lay in the realm of the Persian carpet; he had inherited an eye for the knottage when a corner is flipped to the underside, a nose for identifying the geographical smell of the dye in the wool, a feeling for a deal unsurpassed by anyone in the same field.

Now, among the most famous surviving Persian carpets from Uncle Mehdi's favourite Safavid period, were three weavings known collectively as the Ardebils, and they were created during the reign of Shah Tahmasp. Auntie Gwen couldn't tell us how long ago this was, but said it meant the carpets were pretty ancient. Quite where these masterpieces were made is fiercely debated; reputedly, they were originally kept in a shrine in the town of Ardebil, and hence the name in Persian: Azerbbaijan. But there is no evidence to suggest that the community possessed workshops capable of weaving such things: ordinary carpets, yes – but not these. Whatever their origins, at some point in their history these three gems were bought by Ziegler and Co, a British firm that had set up its offices in Sultanabad in 1880 in order to purchase rugs and carpets for the Western market, and who, once in possession of the trio, did not wish to disclose where they had come from, since, naturally enough, they wanted to protect their source: their secret stream of silken textiles in a land where most water sources are burnt up by the sun. One carpet, Auntie Gwen explained, was displayed as so many hundreds of worn and separate fragments in a museum in America; the second, even more important example was housed in the Victoria and Albert, with limited viewing possibilities due to the steady deterioration of the warp and weft, whilst the third, most exquisite and complete carpet lay, rolled up in all its perfection, under the stairs in Gwen's sitting room. Gorgeous, she said it was, going all poetic: its aged colours made the daylight around it shimmer, as if in anticipation of summers to come. At one end, there was faint evidence of an inscription – Masqud of Kashan 946. This, Auntie Gwen continued with a little smile, knowing how she had impressed us all with her level of knowledge, added considerably to the carpet's already breathtaking value. So why had a business man like Uncle Mehdi burdened his brother and wife with this treasure trove, when – after all – they were instructed to never use it, to never breathe a word of its existence to anyone?

The truth was, Uncle Mehdi had experienced some small difficulties in his recent past, before Auntie Gwen had got hitched up with Uncle Ab. I emphasise this because I wouldn't want you assuming that our family was anything less than above board in moral matters. Mehdi had been in prison – he had done three years in solitary confinement – for acts against the government. Some people we know would say that such acts deserve rewarding but, whatever, Uncle Mehdi had left Tehran penitentiary a scarred man. And, after that, he made up his mind to keep to the shadows, deal low, keep his treasures in other lands, smuggling them in only when the time was right – when every mullah had his back turned, their arses in the air as they bent to pray. The carpet was known amongst Iran's dealers. It was a legend, to be brought out at night, retold and embellished, over and over. Lost, the storytellers would whisper, and Uncle Mehdi would nod respectfully, hug his secret with silent delight. He would die, he had decided, sooner than tell anyone the carpet's whereabouts. Three years in prison had reaped a profit. He had come out knowing where the carpet was. It was his in exchange for delivering letters to an inmate's wife. Such is love. He hummed his favourite Persian love song: *How Can I Live Where Thou Art Not?* Soon, there would be a reason for revealing the carpet, as if it were a trophy bride. There would be a right time, and the right deal. It might take a year, or even ten. Abbas's wife was an ideal caretaker for the time being – somewhat ignorant, but very clean. He would contact them, and Abbas would deliver the gem.

*

After the visit, Auntie Gwen found it harder and harder to ignore the rolled bit of rug under her stairs. It was in the way, for one thing, dislodging the upright piano from its position against the wall, so that the tarnished candelabra jutted out at an awkward angle, creating a sharpness in the room that Gwen found hard to accomodate. The boxes of stored belongings from Mehdi's previous visits – painted pen boxes; baccarat glass decanters, small French hunting scenes – these were now on the first floor landing, piled precariously like children's building bricks the moment before they fell. If they were careful, Gwen argued, why not bring the carpet out, enjoy its beauty as it was meant to be enjoyed? Uncle Ab was not to be persuaded, not immediately anyway, and Auntie Gwen had to threaten to leave with her gondolas several times before he gave in and agreed to help her ease out the large roll, move the old piano back to base. The sharpness of the room smoothed out at last, Auntie Gwen was to enjoy the moments that followed, the slow revelation beneath their feet. Even Abbas got excited then, she told us, something that didn't happen very often. He said his mind became flooded with childhood memories of picnics beneath the chenar trees near the house where he grew up. For Gwen, it was simply colour and light – almost liquid – yes, every detail on it moved, she remembered – every tree, every flower – rising up, into the room. They rolled it up after that, placed it back in its hiding place beneath the stairs. If the piano stuck out, at least now Gwen appreciated the necessity – felt complicit in the admiration of a piece of old rug. From that day on, when Abbas was at work, Gwen would move the piano out, fold out a small corner of the carpet, enjoy its perfections: its magical sheen.

*

About a year later, a group of wise men were enjoying mint tea in a salon in down-town Tehran. Life was good, and the government moderate – encouraging investment in Western ideas, if not yet in Western spirit. Land was the modern currency, and the wise men were discussing the latest trends in holiday resorts. They were the best way to give their children a living – ski resorts in the mountains, beach resorts up at the Caspian Sea, desert resorts for the tourists – one could go on and on. Iran is a big country; its geographical diversity immense. As the conversation expanded – in volume as well as in participants, with Uncle Mehdi arriving about halfway on his way home from a party, it became clear that one of the wise men – the tallest one – had something special to sell. Expensive. Extremely expensive. He didn't expect a quick bid, he announced, closing his eyes. Few would have the resources he required.

As Mehdi pressed closer, along with dozens others, the rumour spread around the gathered crowd that the tall wise man had a mountain he wished to bargain with. And not just any old mountain, since mountains could be snapped up quite easily these days, along with dried-out river beds and pieces of sky, but the mountain known throughout the land as the Koohe Noor. The Mountain of Paradise. The crowd took a sharp intake of breath, in collective disbelief: What next?! But then it relaxed again, and began to laugh – a great big belly-roll of a laugh that rolled around the tea room and halfway down the street. Who the hell could afford such a mountain? What nonsense!

What a wonderful joke! The tall wise man was deeply offended. If anyone wanted it – and it would make a dream resort of any kind; reap profits as yet unimagined – they had three days in which to make their bid. Three days. Three days only, and after that, the tall wise man said, he would change his mind. The crowd loved this little touch; it took them back to the oldest of the olden days – when destiny was always written in stars.

*

Abbas was out in the garden, helping Gwen to repair the fence at last, battered almost to smithereens after the winter storms. They were enjoying the late spring weather; doors and windows left wide open, day after day, enjoying the blossoms and the bird song, and were about to lay breakfast when the fax message came ripping through the calm of the day:

Come today with the child.

They both understood. Abbas had some travelling to do; the piano would find its space once more, under the stairs.

But first, they agreed, they would have coffee and their fresh baguette and Spanish peaches. Abbas would telephone the airport, and then, as instructed, they would unroll the Ardebil; refold it to form a square that would fit more easily into the large suitcase Mehdi had left behind for this purpose. They were to pack on top of it as many of Abbas's old clothes as would be willing to be squeezed and wrung into the remaining space. Finally the suitcase was to be tied around its waist with a fat piece of faded yellow, nylon string. Lucky string, Mehdi had called it – since he used it on all his visits, and no customs officer had ever yet asked for it to be untied.

And as Gwen and Uncle Ab sat there, lamenting the fact that he would now be gone for several days, Gwen thought she heard hatchlings in the wall nearest the kitchen. Our Aunt loved things like that, Gran had told us, ever since she was very young. She put down her coffee and walked slowly – on tip-toe, almost – to where she thought the noise was coming from: in the cracks between the bricks under the wisteria. But no, she said, the high-pitched cheeping seemed to be further away – inside the house, if you can believe it – and somewhere near the piano!

'We've got birds!' she whispered to Uncle Ab. 'Babies nesting in the piano!'

Abbas wasn't that interested; his mind was too occupied with the trip ahead – the fact that, if the string trick didn't work, he might end up in prison, in a country he no longer loved.

'Abbas, come and help me lift the piano lid – quietly!'

He drained his coffee cup, moved slowly towards the kitchen door. The cheeping had stopped. Started up again. 'No,' he said steadily, 'that's not coming from inside the piano. Maybe behind. We have to move it, anyway.'

Gwen insisted they move the instrument very carefully – in case there were birds under it – and she was disappointed to discover there were not. Their efforts had created too much noise and the hatchlings were silent again when the piano finally stood back, revealing the dark, spidered space beneath the stairs, the long body of carpet nudging its way out.

'They're in there!' Gwen clapped her hand over her mouth. 'Get them out then,' Uncle Ab said – something like that, and Gwen had really put her foot down then, said No – they couldn't possibly disturb the young. They would have to wait until they left the nest. They were robins, she announced; she'd seen the adults in the garden, on the doorstep. Hadn't given them another thought at the time, presumed they were nesting in the wall.

Abbas had to send a message after that. His older brother was dining on caviar and melon, in anticipation of the stunning deal that would make him – well, quite literally – king of the Persian Business World, when the fax started ripping through his midday meal:

Baby delayed.

There were no more fax messages that spring, nor visits from Mehdi.

They heard from relatives that the mountain deal left him depressed, without any further appetite for travel. And Auntie Gwen remained unofficial guardian of the carpet; they grew old and threadbare together – Gwen more rapidly perhaps than the costly Ardebil. She had it laid out in the sitting room, much to her husband's horror. It was written in the stars, she would tease her steady Abbas, and he, of course, although he said nothing, was absolutely convinced of it.

The Last Jumpshot

Leonora Brito

Xtra practice? say the old laggers, the old leg timbers
Parish and Bo. You mean xtra on top of xtra?

Well, practice makes perfect, I point out cheerfully.
And anyway, Coach wants us there. For one last run-out.

S alright for you – Captain Fantastic.

Yeah, Mr Campbell Jones!

But what about us, man? says Chip. We're whacked
out.

No! No! I got plenty left in the tank, says Id, the
Valleys' Boy. Let's go for it!

Silence.

I vote we go for it – ?

Everyone looks at the white boy 'gone off'. As if
they've just been dealt a kick to their collective sensitivities.

Then Chip-chip jumps to his feet, suddenly re-energized, resurrected, almost. Yo, let's go, he says, breezing past Id #1, as if Id #1 had never spoken. Come on guys, what're we waiting for, yeah?

The guys jump up. Yo, let's go!

Great, I say. Now we're all agreed.

Bouncing the orange basketball I follow them out of the flat, thinking, smiling. It's because of me that Idris #1 got involved with the A team in the first place, along with his sub and namesake Idris #2. I recommended them to the new Coach, Mulrooney. The two Ids, bible black and paper white. Outside competition. Works like clock.

Standing by the bus-stop. Waiting. Fooling around, waiting, in an afternoon sun that gives off plenty of light, but no heat. Maybe it's too late for heat this time of year. Even so, we six black guys (one honorary) standing on the green hill, under the lone, battle-scarred bus shelter must appear potent. Sunlit. At least in the sunken eyes of elderly shoppers on the supermarket free-bus, which hoves into view before we've been standing there five minutes.

Hey look what's coming, says Chip. *FAZZDERS!*

And the guys start yelling *fazzder! fazzder! fazzder!* as the bus crawls up the hill. The uniformed peaked cap behind the wheel looks as though he'd like to drive straight past. But we step out into the road, all six of us and flag him down. A shade uncool for young gods lately fingered by the sun, agreed. But we can brazen this out. Easy. After all, why pay more, as *FAZZDER* says?

Thank you, driver!

Yeah, thanks, drive!

You boyz all goin shoppin?

We are, drive, says Chip. Gonna buy... washing-powder. Ain we, guys?

S right, yeah. Big bogzz size!

Inside the bus, the chit-chat drops to a murmur as we crowd on board. Then a few bold whispers follow us up. Whispering, all the way up the winding stairs: look... look how many... Somalis?

Innit Somalis?

All praise be to God I say, seeing the upper deck empty; like a breath of fresh air.

Old fogies. Though that type of mis-identification doesn't bother me at all. Because I'm secure in my Keltic-black heritage, come whatever? But it riles the hell out of Parish and Bo, because Parish and Bo are Docks. And being 5th or 6th generation Docks Boyz (from 'Old Doggz' as they kindly explain to the rest of us) means being black in a way that is knee high to royalty. At least the way they tell it. Though Lisha – who knows – reckons the nearest Parish and Bo come to being royal, is when they're sat on their butts in the Big Windsor holding forth. There the guys get serious admiration and respect (from flocks of dare-devil scribes, tourists and whatnots) simply for sitting and being: Old Doggz.

Which is why they feel particularly hurt now, and aggrieved.

D'fuckin dee-crepts, says Bo. I'd like to punch their lights out. One by One.

Yeah, dee-crepts, says Parish. One arf of em are wearin NHS eye-glass an they still carn see! I mean, do I look *Zomali, me?*

The two Ids seated down the front of the bus throw a quick look back. Then they make cartoon type eyes at one another, and burst out laughing. *Zeeong!*

Oi, shouts Bo. What you got to laugh about, *Warrior Boy?*

The cut in his voice is directed at Idris #2, who is indeed Somali, and very tall timber. Which fact perhaps Bo has forgotten as Id is seated. Now the Somali boy shoots his long legs from under the seat and thunders down the aisle of the bus.

I'm Warsangeli, he yells, right up in Bo's face. You get it right, OK? Warsangeli Welsh!

Guys, I raise my hand peaceably. Let's all remember we're a team, OK?

The only response to this is a simmerng, mutinous silence.

And then my mobile goes off. And suddenly everyone is transfixed as this wondrous new ringtone hits the air.

Orr, man, now that is just – just –

Awwsome, supplies Id #2.

Aye, *awwsome!* agrees Bo. I mean, d'fuckin US Cavalry Charge?

S what they use on the NBA clockshot, innit? says Id.

Correct, Mr Hassan. Grinning, I let the mobile play on, unwilling to break its spell. And when Lisha gives up and rings off, the famous US bugle call continues to root and toot in our headspace. Like mood music. Linking us, each and every one of us six guys sat there on the *FAZZDA free-bus*, to the place where we know we wanna be, which is Planet NBA!

Though the bus actually drops us off at the out of town shopping complex. And while the pensioners shuffle forward with their bags and four-wheel trolleys, we're down the stairs, off the bus and out, into the sunshine. Green fields. The guys look round. Birds and shit. For them, this is always, *always*, the back of beyond. But not for me, I grew up here. I'm Pontprennau through and through.

Dotted across the fields are the familiar black and white splotches, sturdy young calves chewing up the grass. It's like those pretty pictures you get on cartons of *Ben & Jerry*'s ice-cream. Except that these are male, Bobbi calves and therefore useless for dairy; but great for kebab meat. Nowadays donner kebab is all these big-eyed spindly legged guys are good for, apparently.

*

So it's Friday afternoon still. And very late in the afternoon for some of us, standing around courtside, kitted up and ready to go. At only 5 feet 8 inches tall, and with the *Big Two O* approaching fast, it's beginning to dawn on me – that I'm only growing older, not taller. While lags like Parish and Bo are even further down the hill.

But right now? Our spirits are sky. Keyed. Because incredibly, this last-minute run-out has coincided with a VIP visit. Up and coming Councillor Ms Susannah somebody, has turned up here at the Sports Centre (actually a discontinued warehouse) with a TV camera crew in tow.

And while the Councillor lady and Coach Mulrooney talk to the cameras about disaffected youth and the need for *blah blah blah*, we await the whistle. Excited, expectant and more than ready to roll. Then, unfortunately the Councillor lady trips over her tongue, and starts talking about *disinfected* youth. And they have to start over again.

Orr, man!

The guys fall out, and begin to goof around a little.

Hi there, whispers Chip, pretending he's on camera. My name is Michael Jeffrey Jordan an I'm not *disinfected*, bold-assed bitch. Y'hear? I'm still catchin!

Yeah, he's catchin, he's catchin –

An we catchin!

Orr, c'mon guys, behave –

OK. Hi, I'm Kobe, whispers Id the Valleys Boy. And everyone cracks up laughing.

Including me. Until I note that Coach Mulrooney, all black beetling eyebrows and Irish-American red face, is looking hard across the floor. At us, at me? Immediately I'm reminded of the need to keep a serious head on here. I mean, once we get to London and tomorrow's final – who is to say who's out there? Watching? But for now Coach Mulrooney, the man who successfully re-branded us from the Karbulls to the Crows (post-9/11) is calling the shots.

OK guys, let's keep it down, now, I say briskly. Just 24 on

the clock, and it will be the *Big One!*

Yeah!

When Kardiff Crows go toe to toe with the London boyz.

D'cocker knee boyz?

Yeah, d'cocker knee boyz! Suddenly I slam the air with my fist and yell out loud: Hey, no con-test!

*

At last Coach Mulrooney blows his whistle. That heart-stopping shriek. And for half a nanosecond I freeze – like a five year old, back on the school playground. Until I break free, shake free from the loop of time and go charging forward –

Great shot there, Campbell! shouts Coach Mulrooney, as we go three on three for the cameras, and I make the first basket.

Great jumpshot!

Then everything spools forward for me. Faster and faster. And despite my best efforts to play it cool, (keep it for tomorrow, play it cool) I'm suddenly on fire. Smoking. The heat is in the house, as they say. And what a fantastic house it is! This echoey space we're running in; this *huge* aluminium walled warehouse, that we still call Goodz 4-U. Once it housed an empire of wonderful, wonderful things: like Nike Classic, Air Force, Converse, Zoomerific; and the sneakers I favour today, which are Jumbo Lift-Off.

And again, we have lift-off, because I'm playing out of my skin! Hey where's the D? shouts Coach Mulrooney, abruptly switching sides. Watch Campbell! he shouts in irritation. Stop *Soup* Campbell! (Is *Soup* some jokey kind of put-down, I wonder, designed to halt my flow?) Too bad if it is. And too late. My feet push off the ground, my arm comes up. I grab the orange rock and it's a steal.

They're stealing it! cries Coach Mulrooney. *They are stealing it*! As Id #1 and I rotate the glowing orange rock between us. Tossing it back and forth, back and forth between us. Like a magic ball on invisible string. Invincible as we gallop up court for the nth time. Throwing a fake on Parish, throwing a fake on Chip. We thunder for the line, dropping Bo's D-fence for dead, as Id #2 pops up on the inside. And I toss the ball to Idris, that tall Somali timber. And get it back *smack*! as I run into space and stop. Right foot slam on the edge of the paint.

All at once, the famous US bugle call rings through my head. Fifteen seconds I calculate coolly, or one last jumpshot. And everyone out there will know who I am. I will alchemize my name Campbell Jones. ID-ing it. Gold-plating it to *Campbell*. Period. Aka the Can Man, aka the first Welsh Black who is destined to blaze a trail through the NBA!

The bible tells us that your old men shall dream dreams, while your young men shall see visions. And when I finally make the shot, the ball leaves my hands and soars through the air. Like a vision. Spinning into space, like a dazzling orange sun that arcs, then fades. Drops and fades... fades... fades. Until... hey, hey hey! *It's BIG BASKET and another three pointer!*

But, I thought I caught a sound back there? As the ball

dropped on its way through hoop and net. *It hit the rim*. It hit the rim! So naturally, I have to try again. And again. Leap on the glowing ball and try again. For the perfect throw, the perfect throw. Until united to a man, the guys grab a hold of my arms, just to make me stop. Stop! Then Coach Mulrooney comes rushing up, and thrusting his angry red peasant face right in front of my eyes, he screams: *Are you crazy, or what?*

I suppose crazy must be the answer. No question. Because when he tells me I'm relegated to the bench for tomorrow's final, all I can think to do, right there in front of the cameras, the Councillor lady and everyone, is to throw my head back. Right back, and just... bellow out my misery, like a bull calf in a field. Then bring my head down hard, in a replicating action and nut the guy... and nut the guy... and nut the guy....

Agoraphobix

Siân Preece

The door to the launderette banged open. A teenage boy bundled in with an empty basket and shook the rain from his black hair.

'*Bonjour, m'mselle!*'

'*Bonjour, m'sieur.*'

A first-ever moustache blurred his upper lip. I ducked my head and rattled the pages of my book, but he didn't want a conversation.

I'd already had a visit from Old Resistance Lady. Today she had recreated a fight or a country dance, leaping and gesticulating, her hat askew and her stockings concertina'd around her birds' ankles. The story had ended with a feast, or some enjoyable dentistry. Her son caused her to weep and sigh, and many of her friends had died by firing squad, or fishing. I nodded non-commitally: '*Ah oui?*'

With her finger to her lips, she reminded me, as ever, that she had been in the Resistance, and her eyes cast about for collaborators behind the dryers. She hissed: '*Au revoir!*' as if it was a code that only we knew.

The boy unloaded clumsy armfuls of damp laundry into his basket. A thick mist boiled from the washing machine; steam and cooking oil. I recognised him from the Moroccan restaurant nextdoor. His washing was all napkins, dish-cloths and rags, transparent with grease; none of the sweet smell of fresh laundry.

'Wash them again!' I thought, but he hoisted the basket to one of the dryers and tipped them in haphazardly, not really looking. I wondered what he was thinking of instead. He slammed the dryer door, slammed it again to be sure, then pressed a handful of coins into the slot.

'*Au'voir.*' A nod.

'*M'sieur.*'

Alone again.

My own washing still had a while to go. I hated doing the laundry. I hated our one-room apartment. I hated France. We'd had a fight about it that morning, and now I hated Ed as well. He was a

selfish bastard

and it was

all right for him; he got out to work, he *talked* to people! I was stuck in this rats' paradise every day but that was just

    my mother talking, could I hear myself? Mew mew
mew

yeah, but

    my mother hadn't followed her man's career around
the world like Tammy-sodding-Wynette, and furthermore

    did I think it was fun for him? He couldn't order a
fucking sandwich here, never mind push his research
forward

    and furthermore

    no one says 'furthermore'

    if he could manage not to interrupt for a

    interrupt!

    for a second, he hadn't spent the last two days
bug-spraying the apartment! The stuff was probably
carcinogenic

    not like my twenty-a-day habit, oh no

but

    no wonder I smoked! It was on my CV under 'Leisure
Activities': smoking, drinking, and trotting after my
husband like a lost gosling

so

    what did I want to do? What did I *want*?

I didn't know.

Alone in the apartment, my own anger wheeled and turned
on me, leaving me shaking. I submerged it in a fit of
cleaning, hating myself for being like my mother, polishing
her frustration into the shine of the dining room table,
justifying herself with her impeccable housekeeping.

I cleaned until even the radio noise seemed untidy, and all that remained was the laundry bag, fat and full. I would have to take it down and wash it.

I would have to Go Out.

Going Out was not a casual undertaking. I wondered if I was becoming agoraphobic. I had an idea that there was a character in *Asterix* called Agoraphobix. Not in French, though: the names were different, like Tintin's dog being Milou instead of Snowy. I would have to go to the library in the Carré Curiale and look it up. Hope no one spoke to me.

To face the journey to the launderette I tooled up with my 'security'. Outsized dark glasses, my cheap knock-off Walkman from Carrefour, a book, fags and matches. There was only one shop in Chambéry that sold British cigarettes; the shop-keeper called me 'Seelk Cut'. I put on my don't-talk-to-me coat, its turned-up collar reassuringly high, and a baseball cap. Last week, a teenage girl had shouted 'Michael Jackson!' in the street and it was possible that she had meant me.

On the way, I stopped to check my reflection in a parked car. The car was too big for the narrow medieval street: a dark dragon, come to terrify the Savoisiens with its mirrored eyes. The rain had covered it with wet beads, shining and rainbowed, a swarm of tiny black beetles over its gleaming sides. I ran my finger through them, and the droplets scattered and regrouped, making a ragged line that pleased me against all that perfection. It enhanced it somehow, like a tendril of hair curled on a bare shoulder.

I drew a swirl around the door handle, marvelling at the streamlining, and peered in the driver's window to see, not my own face, but the car's owner looking back at me.

'*Alors?*'

A young black man, with dark glasses like my own; our noses almost touched.

'*Pardon!*'

I dropped my washing, picked it up again, and shrugged in apology. He laughed, reassured that I was harmless, and gunned the engine to impress me.

I hid in the launderette and watched until he drove away. My embarrassment made me feel hot and sick, but the shrug! I was proud of that shrug. It had felt very natural and French. I was becoming bilingual in body language at least.

Now I rubbed a hole in the launderette's steamy window. The rain had laid off a bit so I went out for a smoke. Smoking was company. Standing in the street looked sad, but standing in the street to smoke had purpose. It was a bad habit like drinking, but you could do it all day. In Chambéry, people smoked everywhere. In the summer, girls lay topless and lit-up by the lake, but my eyes watered at the thought of it: the dropped ash, the give-away matchbooks that spat cinders when you struck them. In the winter they smoked in the supermarkets and food shops. The British tourists, in Savoie for the skiing, would tut and flap, and stamp off to look for 'proper sliced bread' and food wrapped in plastic. We called them 'Eurotrash', but it broke our homesick hearts to hear them speak English.

I whispered the Welsh word for it: '*hiraeth*', and the smoke curled and turned on me. *Hiraeth*. Homesick and then some. Like the song: *We'll kiss away each hour of* hiraeth *when you come home again to Wales*. But Wales wasn't home any more, either. My cigarette burned down. I stood, alone and dispossessed, and it started to rain again.

Back in the launderette I settled down on the clothes-folding table and checked my watch. Ed should be stepping off the bus soon. Five minutes' walk from the terminus, past the Four Elephants fountain, and he would come this way. I'd wave and smile, setting the tone for a reconciliation, for us to talk. We could carry the washing home together. The launderette radio played a song by Les Ritas Mitsouko. I recognised it from the album we had at home and sang along, pleased that I knew the words.

'*On n'a pas que de l'amour; ça non... y a d'la haîne!*' A nice, peppy tune about hate. Catherine Ringer's scratch of a voice reprimanded me:

'*Soyons plus positifs.*'

Positive!

I opened my book and arranged the rest of my stuff around me on the table, my coat and bag forming a nest, a small space for me. I sat in it with my feet up, feeling cosy and self-contained and not unhappy. I'd been down for so long that it surprised me. But I was okay. No one was bothering me. It wasn't an active feeling, I had yet to nurture myself to that state, but it was a start. Ed was right. It was up to me to choose what I wanted.

It was warm in the launderette, and bright, but the oily smell was getting thicker. I hopped up to take a look at the dryer. The boy's napkins flip-flopped to their own dual rhythm in the dark, pitted drum. At their centre was a light effect like sparks, twinkling and starry. They were just starting to smoulder.

'Shit!'

I put my hand to the dryer door, stopped myself. I thought of simply leaving the launderette, escaping, but my own washing was still trapped in the rinse cycle. I ran out to the Moroccan restaurant, faltered halfway when I remembered my purse still on the table, ran on anyway and banged at the back door. The boy was sitting at the kitchen table, carefully cutting pictures out of a skiing magazine, his chin lowered, frowning. He looked up and I shouted: '*La launderette!*' La? Le? No, '-ette', feminine ending, *la*. I shouted again: '*Les serviettes! Vite!*'

He looked confused, then his eyes flicked wide and he leapt up and rushed out past me, the photos whirling in his wake, cut-out arms of paper waving after him.

We skidded into the launderette in a cartoon-panic. The boy dragged the dryer door open and the napkins burst into flames, fed by the inrush of air. He snatched them out, wailing, and we stamped on them frenziedly, wordlessly, dancing in the acrid smoke. They re-ignited like trick birthday candles until we thought of kicking them out into the wet street, where they hissed and floated in the gutter. A woman passing by said '*Oh, là là là!*' and dragged away her dog, who wanted to investigate. The boy stared at the napkins, horrified, turned his back on them and looked to the sky. He didn't want to see them. He turned again, threw his hands in the air: '*No-on!*' – a man's anger with a boy's dark, frightened eyes. I helped him pick through the napkins, looking for an undamaged one that I could offer to comfort him, lacking the words. An older man came rolling out of the restaurant and began shouting at him and, as he did, Ed rounded the corner.

'What the hell's this?'

'There was a fire; we put it out.' I wiped my face with my arm and smelt smoke. Ed wiped a smut from my face. I said: 'I figured out what I want to do. I want to be a firewoman!' I was laughing as I said it, and Ed laughed too.

'Heck, why not!'

The sun had come out, sharpening the smell of the street: grass and wet dust, and pine blown down from the mountains. Groups of children emerged from the school like flowers opening, dressed in bright colours. They shouldered Disney rucksacks stuffed with graph-paper *cahiers*, and chattered with their special brand of authority and earnestness. Ed carried the washing over one shoulder, and held my hand as we walked. Old Resistance Lady came out to sweep the rainwater from her balcony, and a cat on the floor below jumped up at the shower she created and licked his shoulder, outraged.

Back home, we hung the washing on the shower-curtain rail to dry. We ate a makeshift dinner of canned cassoulet, sticky and rich, and finished off a plastic litre bottle of red wine. I speculated on what the boy was doing now....

...his father was telling the story to the customers. It was a big joke; or it was a wicked waste. As the boy passed by in his waiter's jacket, his father reached out and ruffled his hair; or he reached out and cuffed him. Later, in their small, noisy apartment with the green metal shutters, the boy would lie on his bed and plan to run away; or he would dream of girls and skiing, and look in the mirror for his moustache.

It was dark now. I looked for my reflection in the balcony window, but there was only steam from the drying clothes. We drew pictures in it. I drew a stick-man jumping on some burning napkins. Ed gave him a speech bubble, '*Oh là-là!*' We started a window conversation, set ourselves the rule of only using three words.

That poor boy!

These things always. Happen to you.

That was cheating.

I don't care.

I paused and looked at him.

How are you?

I am okay. How are you?

I am okay.

Another pause. He took a slug of wine, wrote:

Fed up here.

Oui, moi aussi.

Let's go Brit.

Go Brit where?

Don't know. Scotland?

Scotland is cool.

Scotland is cold!
Damn cold here!
Yeah, damn right.
I ran out of space and moved to the next window.
You for real?
If you are.
Do it, then?
Do it, then.

The weight of the words became too much; they broke the surface tension, dribbled and ran. In the morning, cold and hungover, I breathed on the glass and the words came back again: 'Scotland?' and a stick man jumping on a fire of napkins and, through the window, snow.

The Fare

Lewis Davies

Naz had been waiting. The clock clicked forward, timing the day, his fare. Rain traced lines between the droplets on the windscreen, tugging each other down. The wipers swept forward then back. He checked his watch, the fare was for four-thirty. He wanted to finish by six. He was hungry. He hadn't eaten for nine hours. He didn't like getting up before it was light to eat. It didn't suit him. The days were longer with no food.

He hoped the boy would eat tonight. It had been nine days now. He could see the heat inside his son as it rose to his skin in sweat. But his eyes were still quiet, looking beyond them to somewhere else. The hospital was clean, white and efficient and it frightened him. The single room that surrounded them, hushed.

He needed to finish. Time to eat. Time to visit.

He turned the engine on. A light in the hallway of the house caught him before he could drive the car away. Then the door opened and a man ran from the doorway down the path to the waiting cab.

A rush of cold air filled the car with the man as he clambered into the back seat. He was out of breath, his coat ruffled up. Naz watched him as he tried to settle himself and his briefcase into the seat. The man took off his glasses to wipe the steam and rain from the lenses. He peered into the front, up at the mirror, his eyes squinting with the effort.

'Crickhowell House.'

The man spoke with an accent that Naz found difficult to pierce.

'Sorry, say again.'

'The assembly building.'

'Ah, no problem. The bay, yes.'

The man just nodded and turned to face away from the mirror.

Naz concentrated on the traffic ahead as he pulled wide into Cathedral Road. The cars were lined tight, nudging each other out of the city for the weekend. This was a city that dozed through the evenings, only coming awake for a brief few hours between eleven and three. Alcohol lowering the inhibitions it pulled tight to itself during the day. The churches still blistered the city, still calling to it through empty pews. There wasn't enough here yet to break with its past.

Naz had lived in Manchester. It was a real city, full of people, full of the swirl of imagination. There were secret

places in that city. Even for him, there were places to drink,
to meet women. It was okay to pay for it then. He had been
a single man. There were necessities he couldn't ignore. He
could remember his friends on the streets at home, holding
hands. Frustration dripping between them and not a
woman in sight. Death and marriage had saved him from
that. His father had always expected him to give in and
come home. The old man was still expecting his son's
defeat when he cut into his leg with a cleaver. An accident
but still death. Naz had looked for the memory, searched
through its corners, even though it couldn't be his. The
street thick with the smell of meat. The gutters running
with rats and the crows ready to pick scraps from the
bones. The panic for a taxi. The blood pouring from the
severed artery as he had seen it pour from so many dying
animals, knowing he was dying. He had escaped that. His
father had died in a taxi on the way to hospital.

The youngest son, he was allowed a chance, a chance
to become himself. His brothers had paid for a marriage
then. Sure he wasn't coming back. Insuring against him
coming back. A proper respectable girl. A good name. Her
family lived in the South. They were cousins of a cousin.
He would have to move from Manchester. Too many
memories, connections for a man about to marry. It was
another city, a smaller city. Cities were the same all over
the world.

There were less cars going back into the city. It was a
straight run, Cathedral Road, Riverside, Grangetown,
Butetown, Docks. He could see the faces and houses

change colour as he followed the river to the sea.

The man in the back shuffled the papers in his briefcase. He caught Naz looking at him in the mirror and smiled unsurely back.

'I'm late.'

Naz smiled. 'Can't go any faster. The traffic.'

'No, don't suppose you can.' He looked forlorn.

'Important meeting?'

The man looked as if he didn't quite understand the question.

'At the assembly?' prompted Naz.

'No, not really; a commission.'

'You're an important man?'

The man straightened himself in the back seat. He looked to see if Naz was mocking him. It was a straight question.

'Er, no I don't suppose I am.'

'What's the rush then?'

The man looked away. He watched the river rush below him and the space where there had once been factories now filled with cleared land. A sign marked the opportunity. 'Open to offers.'

The radio crackled through. Naz picked it up. A voice told him he had another call at the University. He could go home then. Narine would be waiting for him. She had been at the hospital for days. They allowed her to sleep there at first. Waiting. But she couldn't sleep and she just spent the nights staring out across the lights that marked the limits of the city. Naz liked the view from the ward. It was the only thing he liked about the hospital. At nights he could see the towns on the far side of the estuary and imagine what it would be like living there. Anywhere but here now while his dreams struggled through in the bed beneath him. It was a strange country, this. A country trying to find its way. There was nothing he could see that wasn't just smaller than Manchester.

He had taken Narine, the boy and the baby out to the coast last summer. The little boy had played in the waves as if they were something new and unique, especially provided for him. Narine had prepared dahl and chapattis which they ate on a rug placed over the sand. He could feel the stares, unease or novelty, he couldn't be sure but they were stares. They had been easily seen on the stained sand. He had ignored them. The beach was packed: children, kites, dogs, sandcastles, the debris of a day out. Naz had been filled with the wealth of summer, the luck that he sensed had provided him with children and a family. Narine couldn't swim but she went into the water in her suit. Still the boy had played with the ball and the waves had played with him. It had been a good day. He would become a father again in the autumn but that was a long way back through the winter now.

The traffic lights held him on the corner of Bute Street and James Street. An ambulance streaked past. Blue lights flooding the cab. The man in the back leaned over to get a better look at the road.

'I didn't think it was going to be like this.'

Naz looked up at the mirror to see the man's face.

Lines of stress seemed to cut into him.

'It's the time of night.'

'No, not the traffic. The city, this country. I don't understand it.'

The lights allowed the car to move forward. Naz checked his watch.

'What time is your meeting?'

'It doesn't matter.'

The man seemed to collapse back into himself.

'It is your country?'

'Yes, but I can't escape from it.' The man struggled in his pockets for money.

The red edifice of the assembly building rose out of the rain. It was spot-lighted but seemed unsure of itself on the stage. An actor who had fluked a part in a new play but couldn't quite remember the lines.

Naz pulled the car into the lay-by opposite the building. Four pounds forty was displayed on the clock. The man handed him a five pound note. Naz knew he would require change.

'Can I have a receipt, please?'

Naz scribbled through the amount on the back of a card. His writing had never been as good as his speech but he was okay on the numbers. The man pocketed his change and the receipt. He got out of the cab and shut the door. Naz pulled the car back onto the road and headed back into town.

He didn't like calls at the university. They were usually students. There were too many students in the city. The city swelled with them every October, gorging itself on their easy money. But by December he was tired of their jokes, their endless enthusiasm and the way they threw up on his car. Today was the last day of term. He kept up with these events. He used them to mark his time in the city. Six years now. Six years with a new wife and now two children. The first one was a boy, that was good. The next a girl. That was good also but maybe more expensive. Still he loved girls and the way she opened her eyes to him. He would earn enough money. He would be successful in this city. His father-in-law had offered to lend him some money to start a business. It was good to be in business. In business for yourself. He knew about the cars. There would be younger men keen to work longer hours as the city expanded. He wouldn't be a young man much longer. Then he would need to make a business.

The car pushed itself along the fly-over which cut back into the centre of the city. The road rose steeply, soaring above the railway line and the units which lined its route out to the east. From the top the city was all briefly visible before the road crashed into the walls of the prison and the horizon reduced itself to streets again. The traffic slowed him again at the law courts. He wasn't sure if the fare would be still waiting at the university. People called through then forgot about it.

The students reminded him. There had been a ripple of cases last winter. He had seen their faces in the *Echo*. Bright, young, hopeful, dead. It took you so quickly. There had been a man working in a restaurant he had heard about, a Hindu. He had only lasted two days. Everyone had a story. The boy was a fighter. A strong boy. He could feel the determination in his arms as he clambered around his shoulders, mouthing words in two languages. It had been too many days, the dark days of winter in the city. He called back into the radio. He was signing off for the night. There was a brief, strong complaint from the operator on the far side of the call. Then he put the handset down.

He had followed the cars out to the cemetery a month ago. They had been given a plot in Ely to the west of the city. The graves were new. They had been cut deeply into the soft Welsh loam. Each new mound, a life ending out here, many miles from the start in a dusty village on the Indus plain, or the crumbling walls of Lahore or Karachi. The cities themselves had changed their names as if able to disown their children. They couldn't return to a place that no longer existed. They had cut themselves off and would now be the first to die in this new place where it rained through the long winters. He had thought of their hopes. Many of the graves carried pictures of them as young men. Faded, over-exposed pictures of dark men in poor new suits eager for a go at the world. Most had thought they would go back.

They had listened solemnly in the mosque off Crwys Road. The walls dripped with the sounds of his childhood and the cool mornings in Peshawar before the sun got too high. The time to work. His father had been keen on education, avoided politics. The future was commerce.

The new mosque had been a factory making clothes.

They had bought it with donations and optimism. He never attended much himself. The community was growing. He could buy good meat now, vegetables he hadn't seen since he had left Manchester. His wife bought clothes from people who could speak Urdu.

The meat was good but to be avoided, in memory of his father. But it was there. They had some strength now, numbers. The boy would be starting school in a year. He would learn English properly then.

There were casualties. His closest friend ran a chip shop in Llanrumney and was living with a woman called Ruth. He had given up the cars. He was too old for the abuse and the girls who wouldn't pay you and the men who simply walked away. He would trust in Allah, he had claimed, and now he was sending money to a woman he had married and living with one he hadn't. But Naz couldn't leave the faith. It was part of him. The inscription above the door convinced him. Allah is good. Allah is great. And indeed he had been. But now with his son at the hospital he wasn't so sure. The little boy had committed no sin. He remembered his nights on the riverside in Manchester.

He drove the car along Richmond Road, across the junction. The lights favouring his flight. He pulled up at number forty-seven Mackintosh Place. The lights were on in the front room. He could feel the tension in his fingers as he cut the engine and opened the car door. The door to his house was ajar, he could smell the good smells of cooking flood through him. He found Narine in the kitchen.

She was sitting at the table slumped over, her head resting. He touched her hair. She stood up and folded into him. He knew his daughter was being cared for; he knew the boy had gone.

Bin Laden's Hiding In My Liver

Thomas Fourgs

Tavish, white, male, a solitary ambient replenisher in his late to super-late twenties, sneaks early one September Sunday morning to ⊆ₐᴅᵢ♡⊆. *Rather he flops into the broken-off off-licence near the cemetery....* The fridge is at the back and he slides the door for a four-pack of Strongbow (5.3%). He knows thcy can't serve till len on Sundays but he lifts the cool wifebeater all the same. Sadiq's at the till; he's said nothing yet but that too means nothing. Save he stacks battalions of two-litre White Lightning bottles (7.5%) underneath five racks of porn and frowns when someone buys either, or worse, is tempted. *Oh thee who believes take not the Jews or Christians for friends....* He's a miserable cunt. And has been since his two Rottweilers, who guarded the place, got stolen. Now Tavish, perhaps driven by a twisted need to prove that, alkie though he is, in his stained T-shirt (he realised three corners – and six flights – from his stinking flat, when it was too late to go back and change) and ripped jeans (well they were fashionable, at least they were fashionable once upon a time, whatever time this is), he has, nevertheless, some intelligence, more brains than this grumpy money-grubbing fucker at the till, well – he slaps the full weight of *The Sunday Reconnoitre*, with the cider, on the counter.

So Tavish leaves for the cemetery with just *The Sunday Reconnoitre*. He has something like an hour to kill. Sometime in the night he became something beyond porridge: soaking and cold and unable to twitch a limb... limp-dicked, pish-stinking, the drink had exploded like dynamite: smashed glass, lacerations, purple skin, one contact lens in and back to square 0.... Till outside the seagulls began to screech. That dreadful pre-dawn slide of a pish-drenched belt through the straps of Sugar Puffs-smelling wet jeans.... He iced a shower at five am, couldn't care-lessed the washing machine at six. Now as Tavish limps amongst thousands of souls all he can think of is licensing time. For the sixth time along Plot J he realises he has no watch.

He snatches grass between the tombstones. He thinks of golf fairways. Feigning to swing, he imagines playing chip shots from tight lies. Flight it over the yew tree and land it next to the giant vault with the bird on top. Yeah, pin-high. 'Stone dead.' Tavish chuckles. He is looking for a bench, but one that's not in sight – of mourners, not his own vision. 'Although,' Tavish says aloud, holding his sides and blinking, seeing nothing but grass and grave, 'we in this town could undoubtedly benefit from a fuck's sight more mourning.' This too makes him laugh.

Presently he's at a triangular crossroads somewhere near the change-heart of the cemetery. Here three gravel paths collide, trees overarch and there is a bench. He'll lie there using the newspaper – DINOSAUR FOUND IN SUBMISSION RIVER – as a pillow, and dangle his right wrist over his left eye, the left over the right.

Dog-tired.

How will he know when it's ten o'clock? To squint into the sun and imagine its arc through the blue sky, like Crocodile Dundee (though he cheated) with his hat? It's a private triumph to use the full branches of a tree so that now he can look at the sun without shielding his eyes. 'I say... 9:27.' Funnily enough he can guess the time instinctively – and be smack-on – in the dark of the night.

A cartoonist once lived in the flat above him. Well, they said he could tell the time, simultaneously, in twenty different zones. When he left the block all his personalities trooped after him. Cursor Trail they called him (as perhaps his personalities did too – when they thought *he* wasn't listening). Tavish now says quietly: 'Aye, the paranoid cartoonist.' Then: 'Fuckin nut, he was.'

Reasoning now. Everything that lives is altered by time. He part-dreams that time will speed to him, help him alter his brain, which is roasting in the lucky sunshine.

At last he hears a bell. But he can't be sure if this is the first or second strike – if he counts what he thinks is nine, it might be ten, and if ten it might be nine, which will make him at most twenty-seven minutes less accurate than that con-artist Crocodile Dundee! All this he thinks in a blink, counting two, three, four, five, six... eight, nine, ten, eleven, twelve, thirteen.... ('Lord, even the clocks're broken down.') At two-hundred o'clock, shadows of wings sweep up the path. Not so far away, the traffic grumbles have become – suddenly – constant; the sound begins to mar the purity of the bird-song in the immaculate, unvisited cemetery. Meanwhile Tavish is reasoning there is something incongruous in drains sharing land crammed with skeletons. (How'd they find space for everyone?) Tavish decides, rising in a mock athletic sit-up from the bench: 'I must get a drink.' Twenty steps later, after pausing to peer in the bin and find, to his amusement (and he knows it before he looks anyway) – well, the bin is chock-full of empty White Lightning bottles. 'A bloody drink.'

On the street again, back to ꜱᴀᴅɪᴄꜱ. The LCD in the tram shelter tells him it's 9:54. Some wanker huddled underneath it is saying into his mobile: 'Yeah yeah yeah. There's a phone box two hundred metres down the street, when I get there I'll page you....' Tavish encounters a tramp – scraggly grey hair, buttonless coat, a mouth of broken teeth. 'You couldnae lend us some pence so's I can get mysel' a can o' beer?' And Tavish understands. He finds a pound. The tramp grins and follows Tavish into the shop.

'Is it ten o'clock yet?' It's close enough and Tavish buys six cans of Strongbow. *Religions change; beer and wine remain*. Funny how you could buy drink and porn and lottery tickets on Sundays but the selling of Bibles was not allowed. Behind him the tramp puts down a single can of Strongbow.

'I'm no' a copy-cat, eh?' Deep chuckles.

Tavish returns to the cemetery. Or rather the cemetery returns to Tavish.

Consulting the tombs, a bumble bee zums untroubled around him.

Lots of Thomases and Margarets, most of all Jameses. He comes to a grave next to a griddled drain: over rotting skeletons the mock sewer runs. *In the land of his inheritance he was a burning and shining light* – John 5.35. Another James. Born 1907. Died 1944. *Drowned on his way to Russia.*

A match between Partisan Belgrade and Croatia Zagreb slithers into his mind. (This was before it all kicked off.) It hadn't occurred to him then – and how could it? – that he'd be chucking beer bottles on riot-scattered, tear-gassed terraces with thousands of future war criminals. Time changes all things.

Tavish haunts the same bench.

The headache will not go away. Even his sweat is reluctant.

A senescent neighbour took him once to a meeting. Part of her on-going recovery was to save fellow alcoholics, and after four-and-a-half decades of drinking it was easy to discern Tavish's case. With the leopard-like liver spots on the backs of her hands came wisdom, and when sometimes she saw him, staggering about under the trees, ranting, she would sigh and reflect on all the years she herself had wasted in similar despair.

She tugged him by the arm, but he was not reluctant.

They walked lightly through the park, all smiles and gentle laughter. The other side, through the streets, they came upon two snails on the pavement. Tavish stooped, unstuck them and placed them on grass in the nearby garden. 'Ah,' she said. 'They'd get trodden on otherwise,' he said. She tugged him harder then, like some mad aunt: 'I'm going to dig you up if you kill yourself drinking!' But Tavish hadn't lifted the snails because he wanted to portray insincere or false compassion to his neighbour; he put them in the garden because that's what people did. Or at least that's what people he liked to know did, or would have done. Regardless, the moment seemed to strengthen her desire to drag him through the doors of AA.

He wanted, he didn't want. Alcohol bewildered him: he was cancelled with it, cancelled without it. She stepped into the derelict church, and followed the hum, still pulling at his wrist. Just two chairs were free. Someone was testing the volume on a mike: tap-tap with the finger and then 'Hello-my-name's-Fergus-and-I'm-an-alcoholic.' Now that made Tavish laugh. There were smoke-stained scrolls on the walls. The Twelve Steps. The Serenity Prayer. Bullet announcements:

KEEP IT
SIMPLE

LIVE AND
LET LIVE

EASY
DOES
IT

The meeting opened with a 'drunkalogue' (as she whispered), or a 'share'. Tavish's eyes kept in the main to the floor. People (mostly middle-aged men) commented on the share, related experiences with varying degrees of clarity. Someone was talking about the AA tapes he played over and over in his Walkman. He said if he stopped playing them he'd follow his sister to the mental hospital. 'I came here today,' said another, 'thinking please please please let me like these people.' This was something to do with the folk who came but didn't speak. Who took but didn't give. Another said: 'I was sitting on the stairs and I began to cry because I knew that my legs were going to take me to the off-licence.'

The door couldn't wait to come to Tavish.

In the park afterwards she finally asked him. They were sitting on a bench, drinking takeaway tea. For half a plastic cup the subject had been avoided, for nonsense-talk, like why dogs ran after sticks, why parkies preferred to call themselves urban rangers, and so on, but of course her anti-curiosity could not last. He said it wasn't for him. She wanted to know why. He said he didn't want to insult her, but what did he mean? So after more thought, and perhaps the rest of the cup, he mentioned the God-angle, the cultish incantations – 'Hello I'm Joe and I'm an alcoholic,' ('HI JOE') and cult terminology, like 'share' ('Nice share, Joe') – *endlessly applied brainwashing integrated into a way of life…* and thinking drinking a *disease* when in truth – now Tavish had meditated at length about this – alcoholism was powered by nothing more than Pure Fuckin Greed (although he didn't mention this – neither did he say he thought AA was a place for a Who Can Have The Most Fucked Up Nose competition – 'I mean,' he almost said, 'everyone there had a fucked up nose – ').

In the cemetery the cider's worked like a laxative and Tavish, Tavish is now coming to the weary conclusion that he is in need of a shit. Makes a change, he supposes. He rolls his legs off the bench and shuffles behind an ancient cedar. Nearby there are something like laurel bushes – inside a bush he hops. 'Coiling one,' Tavish says, commentating while he squats. Thinking: having a shit: giving life, defacing death (past-life) simultaneously. Of course he has to inspect his creation. Then he tears a leaf from the bush and slides it between his cheeks. He hopes he won't smear the last of the shit all over his arse. 'I'm a fuckin animal,' he grunts.

Now Tavish sits under a tree drinking cider like a rustic tramp. Humming that old XTC song *Are You Receiving Me?* He is alone, still, in the cemetery. Or rather he is alone but for one man, who passes at a distance with flowers. Closer, Tavish scrutinises a fly on a strip of sun-bleached pine bark, rubbing its front legs with glee. Did it know of the turd or did it think it was Michael Owen? What noises emanated from its fuckin sucking mouthpart?

Finally he stands, stretches, a two-limbed pine looking up and yawning at the two-hundred year old trees.

The tramp has his ID wrapped in cellophane, and he waves this now in the air. 'I don't look forty-seven, do I?'

They're perhaps a distance from the broken-off off-licence, but they've run into one another again. The tramp is drinking the last of a different can. Tavish wonders at the coincidence and says nothing. The tramp smiles.

'Have another personality.' Tavish hands him a new can.

'You're a gentleman, sir.'

'Nah, I'm just a drunkard.'

'So ye are!'

They drink for a bit, watching the traffic. Somewhere not so far away they can hear the sound of Irish accordions, a penny whistle, a mandolin. Tavish thinks dreamily of fighting dogs and thick smoke, red-haired barmaids and shamrocked Guinness.

'What's your name, son?'

'Tavish. You?'

'James.'

Tavish laughs, says: 'That connects.'

James is from Glasgow. He lives out of bins. He never gets hangovers because he has this magical ability to manufacture cans.

'Have you many friends, Tavish?'

To Tavish, this is a horribly acute question. It feels scripted. For a moment James takes the form of a second spirit.

'Well,' says Tavish, 'they're dwindling.'

He hasn't heard him. Maybe.

'Hello there!' James greets another passer-by. He is ignored.

'Bit of civility never cost nothing, eh?' James says to Tavish.

'Can you dance the swords, Jimmy?'

'You've got humour, eh?' James says. He asks Tavish if he has travelled. Tavish thinks he means abroad and lists a few places. James cries: 'Woo-ah! Slow down!' He means *travelled*. James has been in eight prisons. He can list them. But instead – and without provocation – begins a frantic rant: 'Matthew, Mark, Luke, John, Acts, Romans, Corinthians 1, Corinthians 2, Galatians, Ephesians, Philippians, Colossians, Thessalonians 1, Thessalonians 2, Timothy 1, Timothy 2, Titus, Philemon, Hebrews, James, Peter 1, Peter 2, John 1, John 2, John 3, Jude, Revelations!' gasping for breath, as if coming up for air, exhilarated in its completion.

'No James?' Tavish says.

'Aye, there's a James,' James says.

Tavish grins and breaks away from his can: 'Hydrogen, helium, lithium, carbon, nitrogen, oxygen... mag-fuckin-nesium – ' he laughs, he can go no further.

James says: 'Is tha' right, eh?' He says: 'I just buried me mother.' Five or maybe three times he tells Tavish this, and Tavish, swaying, his back now to the railings, blinks, wondering how long this man has just been burying his mother. How many years?

'Time for the offy,' Tavish says, pushing himself away.

There, he tells James to wait outside (he does) and picks two four-packs from the fridge, one for James, one for himself. Tavish comes from the shop and hands James a bag.

'Happy Christmas.'

'You're a gentleman, sir.'

'See you later, Jimmy.'

Tavish begins to trudge down the street. There is one last yell before they part forever (or at least until next Sunday): 'TAVISH!'

Tavish turns and waves, and then ducks under a bridge.

Monday morning Tavish calls Mammoth, his place of work, and says he's sick. He doesn't care if no one believes him, because he *is* sick. Physically, mentally, emotionally – he has the set. He could put hotels on them. His flat stinks of pish and vomit, and he'll pay anything to retreat a few days. Tenuous: his psyche. Lowering the receiver Tavish is again amazed by his scheming endurance, that he has lasted so long without being rumbled. Though he has to backtrack a little in this instance, since it is impossible (he reasons) for him to get his mattress down six flights of stairs (he can't imagine being caught in the lift) and into the street without anyone seeing him, clocking the stench, its wretched circles of disappointment.

Hey, pride... hey, shame. He has sat on a chair and stared at his bed with his head in his hands. Look at the pish on that fuckin thing. Look at that fuckin pish!

Like he had woken one morning to see it was all too good, and had from that moment subconsciously raised a sledgehammer and begun smashing his world to pieces – and only now were the shards hitting the glass walls and shattering into still smaller pieces...

And look at those come bubbles. Remember, son? Two coats together, two watches by the bed, scratches on your back – remember how you used to fuck? He has wished the smell away. He has thought about curling the mattress and pushing it out the window, but then it, being a double, however wasted these days, is unlikely to squeeze through the frame, and even if by some miracle it did, it'd land – after perhaps some seconds of free-fall bliss – only in the square communal garden below, and then he and his infernal mattress would be seen by people on all four sides of the block.

Now he earns a low wage for someone his age (not surprising really since all he does is stack fruit). He cannot afford expense – but what can he do? Go on sleeping forever in that stinking bed? Look at it, son. Look at those glued clouds of urine smudged forever to your bed. Look at them. Some of them overlap. That pish, that pish that came from your uncontrolled bladder while you snored horribly porridged – be thankful you didn't find shit had dribbled out too. Tavish puts on his shoes and heads to the offy for a couple of cans, just to get his balance back. But having drunk half of one he decides to hire a van.

He finds Aardvark Autos, a half hour's walk in the hot sunshine from his flat. The pavements are clogged with pushchairs and people who stand still and drift. It is a hellish trudge inside the brutal landscape of a diseased city, lightened only near the underpass where he stops for a moment and watches teenagers in baggy jeans and T-shirts skateboarding down the ramps and steps, the idea seeming to be who can be first to break an ankle in the most casual way. More concrete, more dog shit, another rubbish skip, another scattered pool of cubed glass from an ex-driver's side window.... He stops at a newsagents for a

Red Bounty to give him energy, a sugar boost, which he forces down and does not enjoy. It's only when he's in the office that he realises he may have been 'seen' during his stumble here, in which case he'll be in trouble at the supermarket when he once again finds himself in a state favourable for work.

There's some tumpy at the counter wanting to know every single thing about the car and the insurance and the mileage and the tyres and crashes. The air conditioning in the office isn't working. Neither is the fan. And still the fuckin tumpy wants to know more. Thinks Tavish: I'm cooking in this fuckin office listening to a fuckin tumpy cunt ask preposterous questions – 'Just take your bastard car!'

At last he's seen, and yes, the mini-van on the forecourt is free. Only the office is now closing and he'll have to hire it for the whole day, bring it back tomorrow morning at seven-thirty. She swipes his card and he scribbles at the foot of some multi-pages without thinking, stuffing the yellow copies in his pocket. He takes the keys and cagily drives away from Aardvark Autos. The mini-van has no back window and he must see with the wing-mirrors. It's not easy to get used to, especially in a hire car he can't afford to bump – 'If you elect not to choose the waiver you will have to pay the first £500 repairs in the case of an accident,' she said – and with a brain full of bees.

Tavish aims for the industrial park. There has been an accident on the highway and the traffic is snarled round the mini-roundabouts where cars jam three abreast. Much hooting of horns and yells out the window. Tavish's got the air conditioning on full blast but still he's sticking to the seat. Pawing the sweat from his face he pleads for this agony to end. 'Soon it will end,' he says, over and over. So he endures forty minutes in the traffic before reaching the industrial park. There, he gasps, when, through the window he realises his fortune and spies a bed shop. He parks, staggers out and into the store and demands the cheapest double mattress. The salesman gives him a price of £105 which seems a bit steep. 'You could get one for £50 if you shopped around, I admit,' he says to Tavish, 'but they'd fall over just like that,' and he flops his hand, as if gesturing impotence.

'Ah, just give me it,' says Tavish, taking out his card.

'Get in there yer cunt,' he says five minutes later, stuffing the mattress into the back of the mini-van.

'But at least I'm making progress now,' he tells himself in the wing-mirror.

'Part 2 accomplished.' Big sigh.

'Christ.'

Back at the block he takes a little while to leave the mini-van. ('Fuck's sake.') Then, with a giant sigh, chanting 'Soon it'll be over,' he unlocks the back doors and draws the new mattress out. With blind determination he then trawls it into the building, the lift, and up to the third floor. He manages to drag this mattress into his hideous lair without anyone seeing him – or at least anyone who'll remember seeing him. (The woman from 1C, the one with the three poodles – Silence, Suburbs, and Sometimes – never speaks to anyone.) But this he takes as a bad sign – now

he's *bound* to be seen going down. Anyway, regardless, he
has the new mattress in his stinking flat. With the windows
wide open and the old one gone, it will soon be habitable
again. He hopes. He knows. Part 3 accomplished. Now for
the most soul-destroying bit. Furiously he attacks the old
mattress, kicks and punches it to the door. On a whim he
decides to gamble on the lift. To his horror it stops on the
second floor.

Like the farmers who dump carcasses of dead animals
in ponds, streams, forests and on roadsides, rather than
bear the cost of their disposal, with their ears cut off to
avoid identification. Like the fox who chews off its leg to
get free from a trap.

Before the doors open he shuffles to hide behind his
mattress, crouching, almost, so that whoever gets in won't
see his head. The doors open. He hears two voices, two lots
of feet approach, then retreat – 'The next one.' The doors
close, the lift descends, Tavish splutters up from the acrid
stench of cooked pish. 'That I should be sunk to this.' On
the ground floor now, and a spirited, tunnel-visioned rage
to the mini-van. He feels it's like disposing of a body, and
in a way it is. He tells himself this is the old Tavish he is
stuffing in the van. Once he's dumped it, he can start
afresh. He will be brand new. He's on the wagon from now
on. No more drinking.

No way.

Into the snarl-up again, air conditioning full blast,
sweating like a rapist. He has an idea that the dump is
somewhere near the industrial park. If only he knew a
different way to find it (a blind man in a gold mine).

He doesn't find the dump. But what he does find suffices. It's a dead-end lane, with industrial yards and buildings on one side, wasteland on the other. Reaching the dead-end, executing an unnecessary five-point turn, slowly coming back the way he's come, Tavish reasons he'll dump the mattress here, there in the stingies on the side of the lane. As he's thinking this a car approaches. A sun visor across the top of the windscreen with

CLEMENTINE

on it. She has her window down and she's smiling. A nice face. It seems she's taken the wrong turn too. There's a little kid in the passenger seat.

Light-headed, and without thinking Tavish croaks through his open window:

'Come and feed the ducks with me.'

'What?'

He says: 'I'm lost.'

Tavish is pins-and-needles-curled on the floorboards by the radiator, pleading for sleep and no more fire in his brain, which is frazzled. He drifts in and out, until sometime round four he jolts: is he dreaming or has something happened? It takes maybe six or two or five seconds for him to focus his mind, which is unusual. Gingerly he pats his legs: thank fuck he hasn't swamped. A thought: mini-van: seven-thirty am drop-off time. Then he has an idea. He rolls over and blinks into the dim orange light for his bag. He tugs it towards him, temporarily contented by its weight. Inside there are six bottles of Scrumpy Jack (6%). Gradually the idea becomes quietly sensational.

Twenty minutes later he is in the street looking for the mini-van. The street is empty and dark. Just past the dead of night, the time when concrete groans. At the van, now: Tavish circuits it looking for hooligan imprint. Like a predator. There is no damage. Key in the lock, lights on, and – with one more sigh – meekly away from the kerb. Again he's thankful there's no traffic (he forgets he can't see out the back). So he chugs the streets to Aardvark Autos. He parks in a larger space further from the forecourt, climbs out muttering obscene gratitude, and fades without once looking back.

He sits on the tree-lined pavement with his back to the wall. He has opened his bottle on a mosque fence, and now he drinks. He thinks of a church recently turned into a porn cinema. He thinks of churches being turned into mosques.

But here the terraced houses are three storeys high. No one lives in them. They are all offices of a kind. Tavish sighs.

No one comes by. He is relieved. Content.

Thinking about the time he lapped ice cream while balanced on his father's knee and his father said: 'Just you enjoy it, son. Because before very long you'll find there is very very little to get excited about.'

This is the time of day when you can *hear* the gulls flying, to perch on chimney pots, atop orange mushroom-like houses and laugh, as if pinching someone's nose over and over... till the first tram, and the wood pigeons....

This is their time: the time of clear skies and silent,

feathered traffic trails against the blinking stars. Every line is a session, every session a line, Tavish thinks....

The church clock chimes seven-thirty, he wanders back to Aardvark Autos. On the semi-lit inside forecourt a man is manoeuvring a transit van. He hobbles after Tavish to the mini-van, takes the keys, checks for fuel and dents, scratches, and says: 'Okay, mate.' Tavish wanders off, swinging his empty bag. (Part 5 accomplished.)

At the corner he changes direction and heads for the broken-off off-licence. Weekdays they can sell drink from eight onwards – not absurd Sunday's ten – and he has some childish desire to challenge the shop owner again. Tavish remembers a train trip to Southampton. He'd taken a seat opposite a woman who blanked him right away: she turned her head and stared through the window. Tavish, suddenly self-conscious, had looked down at himself, then, and scrutinised his clothes. No, he thought, he was okay – why had she taken an instant dislike to him? From his bag he removed a can. The woman tutted. It was a leisurely drink, and when he reached down for a second, the woman visibly shivered as if she was wearing eighteen million pairs of gloves, and grumbled something he did not catch. (Bitch.) A delicious menace came over Tavish. He drank this second can a little quicker and was faster stooping for a new one once it was gone. And so he accelerated through his tins, drinking faster and faster, gulping now instead of sipping, belching noisily behind his hand, faster and faster, faster and faster, amusing himself playing Appal the Old Woman as the train rushed down the bloody map. By about can nine he was sucking up dregs and blowing off froth at the same time. And then she'd started talking to him, opening with that line he was often asked on trains: *'Are you a squaddie?'*

Now Tavish enters the broken-off off-licence. He's aware it's him alone who'll consider the encounter with gnome-like Sadiq a confrontation – but that doesn't matter. (*The blind and the seen are not equal....*) The trudge from Aardvark Autos has been made pleasant just by the thought.

'Is it eight o'clock yet?' He can't resist a smirk. It's 7:50 but he's got a bottle left in his bag, and he can return to the cemetery while he waits for time to become his friend. Of course the man does not remember him, but that is also irrelevant.

Back at the flat he meets his neighbour. She is testing a new night-latch on her door. Her husband was an electrician who tied cables round ferrets then sent them down narrow cracks. Alas, he is dead. (Terminally inconvenienced as the forces'd say.) Consequently she feels vulnerable.

'Been busy?' perhaps she says.

'Been out collecting,' Tavish answers. He hesitates, bold on the cider, trying to suss if she *knows*.

(*Clunk.*) 'There,' she says.

'The old one's dodgy, eh?'

'You never know what psychopaths are about these days, do you?' she says, and that gets his mind racing. Is she making indirect reference to him? Does she know?

Inside his flat he sits on his new bed and thinks: *'Been busy?'* Busy with what, busy with fuckin stinking mattress? She being sarcastic? She usually sarcastic? '*You never know what psychopaths are about these days, do you?*' She think I'm a psycho? Why'd she put 'do you' on the end of it – '*do you!*' She's talking about me. Fuckin ell she knows. But how can she know? I didn't see her. Stands to reason, son, she saw *you*. Tavish stands in front of the mirror and erupts into fragile laughter. He's got some pip or seed stuck between his gum and tooth – but hey, what the fuck. He's got a new bed.

Tavish does the stupid Hollywood thing and straddles a chair with his arms over the back, and considers his new bed. He imagines Clementine speaking to him about it. He can see her, *there*, right there, busying herself with fitted sheets and duvets while she nags:

'You might cut the plastic off it,' perhaps she says.

There's a warning about the plastic packaging the mattress.

'Pah,' he says, and she turns to him, still trying to be optimistic, carry them through the coming argument.

'It's probably for babies,' maybe she says.

He contemplates the bed, thinking: It'd have to be a gutsy little pig to eat that much packaging: a gutsy little cunt to eat that much packaging: it'd've have to be a gutsy little pig-cunt to eat that much packaging: pig? cunt? The warning is for future policeman; the warning is there to save the lungs of two-year-old future policeman. He sneezes with laughter, and the secrecy of it makes her snap – she has decided that he's laughing at *her*!

'Ah, happy days,' Tavish sighs, moving towards the trilling telephone. Without thinking he answers it.

'Hello.'

'Hello Gerald, how are you?'

'There's no one living here called Gerald.'

'What number's this then?'

'45-09-81-66.'

'I didn't dial that number. I dialled my auntie's number: 70-87-00-73.'

'Okay, see you then.'

'Bye.'

He's plays with the fridge magnets, wondering if it really happened. He thinks he'll watch some telly.

So he flops on the sofa. He looks at the can of Symonds (7.2%) in his right hand, wondering if he can be fucked to drink it. Suddenly he feels sleepy. He flips through the channels at least twice – cooking programme… cooking programme – before resorting to Teletext to see what's on. 10:00 C4 *The Land That Time Forgot*. To kill time he scans the news. That cunt Bin Liner's still at large. And sport headlines. Something on top about motor racing (*yawn*). S'only interesting when someone crashes. He fast-texts to 410 for the footy news. Cambridge manager's been sacked… Can't stand adverts. Back into Teletext to see if there's any porn showing later on C5. Dunno. Can't tell. Mind, there's a documentary at eleven o'clock about how different people are in public life to what they're like in their private life: *To Act Or Not To Act*… how many fuckin adverts? Tavish cracks his can.

The Land That Time Forgot. The thing about this film is s'not real. This bit at the start, when the bloke's in the boat with the blonde. I mean, come on, Tavish thinks – the ship's just been blown up, they're the only survivors, they'll either burn to death or get butchered by the Kraut subbers, or at least die of thirst (or be scoffed by sharks), and he's there in the boat and he doesn't even try to get her tits out. Come on, any normal bloke would've got her tits out. And she'd've sussed the situation and probably expected, no – been *disappointed* – if he didn't try to get'm flopped and have his paws truffling into her panties. Come on, they were both about to die!

The dinosaur scenes also make him laugh. He wonders: why do these huge carnivores just stand up, waggle tiny arms and offer huge soft bellies for the gun shot? No way would they've evolved to masters of their own continent with such stupidity. Here, all the giant predators do is growl. Now if I was writing this film, Tavish thinks, I'd have one of the heroes clamped between Dino's toes, and then make Dino slowly munch half a dozen eucalyptus trees, and then have him shit on his face...

Tavish falls asleep.

He should think about ambient replenishment. If he goes to work, and survives, be okayed to carry on, he'll be back on track: Part 6 accomplished and Game Over. Hmm. 'How undrunk am I?' Tavish wonders, lying on the sofa. 'What've I had? Two, three? That's nothing. A nice bath, a big lunch, lots of coffee and Extra Strong Mints and I'll be right. Go back in around three then.' He will be more than okay by three. And of course, *of course*, he's seeing Clementine tonight.

On the back of an envelope Tavish sketches:

work = severance from offy

Chuckling. He'll turn the tables on his position. He'll use work as an aid.

So after the bath and the big lunch he takes the 237 to Submission River, which is somewhere near Mammoth. (He can't take the 222, it's not running. On the shelter's LCD runs round and round: ☹ WE APOLOGISE FOR THE CANCELLATION OF TRAM 222. THE DRIVER'S CAB IS INFESTED WITH FLEAS... ☹ WE APOLOGISE FOR THE CANCELLATION OF TRAM 222. THE DRIVER'S CAB IS INFESTED WITH FLEAS... ☹ WE APOL –). Tavish is clever now. He has the sense to always keep a spare boilersuit clean and ironed – to account for such possib-probabilities as those experienced on the weekend. Tricks of the trade: wino self-preservation. Before that first glass he must see some days ahead. If he is to momentarily enjoy going to hell, he must at least *try* and ensure that the rebound is as painless as can be. Last weekend he was, of course, surprised by the depths of his degradation. That said, the outcome could have been worse. And had the business with the mattress never happened he'd've never had a date at the duckpond, would he?

Over the bridge and into the car-park; he thinks of turning tail but resists the temptation and heads into the supermarket. In the loading bay he finds Mike sitting at a computer pretending to log stock. Tavish hangs his coat in his locker and looks about him.

'All right, Mike. These pallets to go?' Tavish puts his hands on the trolley.

'I thought you weren't due in till four,' Mike says.

'Yeah, well,' says Tavish, 'I came in early to help out. Show how keen and committed I am.'

'Petals won't pay you the extra hour, you know that?'

'I know. Where is he anyway?'

'He'll be in later. It's Day of Atonement or something, apparently.'

'Really? I thought that was yesterday.'

'Uh? Oh yeah. Huh.'

'Was he all right about yesterday?'

'Not really,' Mike says.

'He's never been all right with me.'

'That's because you answer back. He can't tame you, you're too stroppy.'

'Did you say take or tame?'

'And he thinks you're cynical.'

Tavish laughs out loud. 'Mike, there's a very fine line between being taken for a cynic who can't take orders and one who accepts being treated like shit.'

'Petals'll see it differently.'

'He always does.'

'Especially as Melanie reckons he reckons he saw you stumbling round Salac hammering cans at six o'clock in the morning.'

'What? Yeah, right.'

'That's what Melanie says.'

'Yeah, and what was *Petals* doing prowling round Salac first thing in the morning?'

'Suppose you got a point there,' Mike says. 'Do you want to see something spooky?'

'What's that then?'

'Look at this,' Mike says as Tavish comes to stand at his shoulder, 'you know those – hey, you been on the beer today?'

'God, fuck, can you smell it?'

'You reek, mate.'

'I've had a million Extra Strong Mints.'

'Go and chew some garlic. There's some on the veg pallets.' Tavish skulks off looking for the garlic. Presently he returns and begins to peel a clove beside Mike.

Mike says: 'You know those planes that were hijacked?'

'What about them?'

'One of them was Flight Q33, wasn't it?'

'Was it?'

'Now look at this, it's fuckin spooky, man.' Mike types Q33 on to the screen.

'So what?' says Tavish.

'So what? Look what happens when I change the font to Wingdings.'

On the screen blinks:

'Now tell me that's not spooky?'

'Ah,' Tavish scoffs, 'you probably got the wrong flight number.'

He begins to draw the trolley to the door, but Mike stops him. 'No, don't bother with that, mate. If you want to help, go and help them facing-up. You can put that stuff out later.'

So that's what Tavish does. Facing-up is the last thing the replenisher (he believes calling himself an *ambient* replenisher is a tad pretentious) does before the end of a shift. It means ensuring all the Baked Beans labels are facing out, facing the customer. Petals considers it the most important part of the job because if the wrong item sits above the wrong price marker then Trading Standards can fine the store £5000. If you want to get in Petals' bad books, put the cans of tuna where the salmon should be. But today Tavish wishes to do nothing but get his head down, and survive. His recent absence will be forgotten in a few hours, and then everything will be hunky-dory. He can get on with his life. He is in a philosophical frame of mind, then, as he joins the quads Ken, Len, Ned and Ben halfway down the soup aisle.

After a while Tavish is aware that, despite everything, he is fond of humanity.

'We're all vulnerable, aren't we?' he says aloud. 'We're all broken to some extent, aren't we?'

'Tav's being weird again,' Ben tells Len.

'No, come on,' says Tavish, 'it's true. We're all broken. We all rattle a bit.'

Ben tears at the plastic covering a tray of Scotch Broth. He glances at his brothers, then begins straightening the tins on the shelf. There's a Special Offer on Heinz soups. 3 for 2.

'We're all vulnerable's what I'm saying,' says Tavish, helping him with the cans. 'And the funny thing is, if we weren't vulnerable we wouldn't be human. If we didn't rattle a bit no one would like us. Because we'd be too perfect.'

'Your oral hygiene ain't too perfect,' Ben says. 'Fuck me. Go and play with the toothpaste.'

Tavish thinks he's doing fine until some time after four when he gets a call that he's wanted in the loading bay. There he finds Petals. Twenty-something, clean-shaven Petals in his shiny shoes, in his Mammoth suit and tie – Petals, holding a walkie-talkie, standing adjacent to Mike who is now logging stock and definitely not chipping e-mails to his blue and green-eyed girlfriend in Malmö. Petals is the kind of person who waits for the phone to make one last complete ring before lifting the receiver. He doesn't speak when Tavish enters, merely nods. Tavish follows his gaze... and troops mournfully to his locker. A black bin liner is hanging off the handle.

'I'd like you to be out of here in two minutes,' says Petals. 'If you're not out of here by then I'll call someone from security.'

Tavish recalls the interview. He was given a bin bag just like this and told to make a suit from it. Then, to get the job, he had to wear it while improvising role-play with good and bad customers.

'And that's it? No explanation?'

Petals says nothing.

Tavish draws breath and opens his locker. He tugs his jacket off the hanger and doesn't know whether to put it on.

'Your uniform you can return tomorrow. I don't need to remind you that failure to return it will result in a suspension of severance pay.'

Tavish freezes, flinging knick-knacks into the bag.

'Fuck's sake, come on – '

'I've said all that I need to say,' says Petals.

'This isn't very charitable of you, you know... no. You're a fuckin hypocrite, aren't you, pal? You – '

' Security – '

' – You ponce around church – '

' – Someone to the loading bay – '

' – With your fuckin personalised number plates and your fuckin hymns and fuckin car boot sales and fuckin craft shows, and poncey apple pies and village fêtes and all that stuff, and you haven't got an ounce of compassion in your living soul. Not one single bastard ounce. You probably wear cords on your day off! Genesis, Exodus, Oba-fuckin-diah – '

There is a time for all things, and a thing for all times. The thing for this time is a pint of Guinness (4.1%). But one is never enough. So he drinks first in The Hanged Parrot, and then afterwards, further down the banks of Submission River, in the newly refurbished Pointless Exchange. Then a quick triple vodka in The Smouldering Bone. After these miserable drinks he side-steps into an offy and takes a clutter of tinnies ('a carry-out' as Clementine calls it) to the duckpond.

There is still enough daylight for him to see the ducks, but they aren't interested in his bread. He sits with his back to the black railings twirling the wrapper of his loaf, contemplating ungratefulness. It's ungratefulness that hurts the most. But it's a calming experience to watch the light fade (he thinks), or at least it is when no human beings are involved. The green grass, splodged and tickled here and there with turd and feathers, slowly colours black. He pulls on a new can of Tantalum super lager (8.4%) and coos quietly for the ducks.

'They're stuffed,' perhaps pipe-thin Clementine says to him. 'They feed too much on Sundays when mothers and fathers bring their children here. It'll be Thursday before they're right again.'

They watch the baby waves rising and falling on the duckpond.

'How's little Jimmy?' he says to her.

'He's fine.'

'He's with the babysitter, eh?'

'Aye.'

Tavish faces Clementine. He watches her play with the ends of her shoulder-length auburn hair. She's not got her eyes on him.

'I imagined you as Irish.'

'No, from Glasgow, me.' The way she says it: 'Glass-co.' She looks at him. 'Would you be fond of garlic by any chance, Mr Tavish?'

'And your uniform,' she says, 'is that the height of fashion just now?'

'What's wrong with it?'

'It's dire.'

'You should see me get into it,' says Tavish. 'I've got to stand up, like this... bend over, wriggle a bit, fling my arms – it's like trying to break out of a chrysalis.' He slumps back to the grass. 'If you're not drinking, shall I find you some coffee or something?'

'The doctor told me to cut out the caffeine. There's meant to be huge pike in there.'

'In the pond?'

'No,' says Clementine, 'in the fuckin stinging nettles.' She looks over the water. Says: 'I might have to get someone else.'

'Eh?'

'The babysitter. She came early tonight, said if she was a bit late – coming back – it'd be because she got held up at Mammoth. I says to her, "If you're going to Mammoth would you take these bottles down the bottle bank for us?" She says: "Would you like me to take your fuckin rubbish out for you too?"'

'She never.'

'Aye, she did. Sarcasm, eh. The lowest form of wit.'

'Shall we walk for a bit?'

'Can you still walk?'

'They'll close the gates in a bit.'

'Parkies...'

'They're not parkies, they're "urban rangers".'

'Is that right?'

'Or go and see a film,' says Tavish.

'I don't do films.'

'Or a drink.'

'No.'

'What then?'

Clementine says: 'Just sit quietly and watch the ducks.'

Tavish tries to look for the ducks but there are no ducks. Beyond the pond the trees blacken against the pale blue sky, the shrubs are already dark...

In the park (dreams Tavish) – staring out out out as a church bell chimes chimes chimes. Birds beneath our feet. There are sounds of alarm from the birds in the trees, where squirrels move like breezy leaf shadows up the trunks, vanishing before they are there. We are still staring out out out, though all sights are exaggerated, all sounds are exaggerated... Staring and seeming to see nothing but the terrifying problem of being a bear...

He pictures Clementine's legs scissoring his back like tram wipers.

'What fuckin ducks?'

Suddenly Clementine stands. Then: 'I'm away for a pee. Is that all right?'

'Might be,' he says, partly relieved.

He can drink without scrutiny now.

'Like a good boy, eh?' he says, but of course she doesn't answer.

He has his arm round Clementine's shoulder, and they are humming happily out of sync and tune. She asks if he's trying to strangle her and he's holding anti-hiccup breath and then saying: 'Wha'?' They've come to the estate. Here, cop cars creep emergency circles before acting, trying to decide if it's safe, if it's a trap. Which means they tend to react too late. Or at least this is what Tavish tells Clementine. It's not like that at all (well...). But he wants to ensure she's disappointed *before* they reach his flat. This way she'll be more likely to come inside (he reasons), because the surprise – reality not being what she imagines – will *bring her up*. He lives (he says) in a flat on his own, but the walls are so thin he shares with a score of half-people he never sees. 'Save the electrician's widow,' he tells her.

'Is this it?'

Clementine's skin seems grey. He snuffles in her throat. 'I wanna eat you piece by piece.'

'Steady.'

He takes her hand and draws her into the foyer. After months or days of darkness someone has screwed a bulb into the flex. The timer switches are so stiff they can't be switched off, however.

'The woman in 1C breeds tortoises,' Tavish tells Clementine. 'The males butt the females to stimulate them for sex. People complain because the shells keep clacking.'

'Does she really keep tortoises?'

'No.'

She lightly butts him. Tavish begins to glow. At last, a slice of happiness....

So he and Clementine take the lift to the third floor. Between 2 and 3 they kiss. It's sloppy and out of focus, and Tavish gets his face imprinted with buttons.

He tugs her through the doors before they're fully opened. They take the left-side corridor.

He freezes.

She drops his hand.

Outside his flat door is a stinking, pish-soaked, come-blotched, fuckin A-grade humming mattress. The peculiar light through the fire-exit doors shines on the smudged outlines of its pish circles. They can smell the monster from where they stand. Or where he stands. Clementine has disappeared.

Broken, he approaches the small note that is pinned to the mattress:

| Delivered 4am |

Tavish howls.

He jumps behind it, flees into his flat. Slams the door. Rushes from kitchen to bathroom to bedroom to lounge and back again, howling with his head in his hands. Surely it can't be. It cannot be. Not again. No, no, not again. Please not again...

But on the table are some keys. And on the key-ring hangs a cartoon aardvark with the most demented grin on its face.

He stares astonished at his treasure. The aardvark's grin blinks on and off at him.

Tavish turns to his ansaphone and presses PLAY to halt the torture. The message is garbled, but through Tavish's super-sensitive ears it cuts loud and clear:

'*Wee Jimmy McTavish! Will you nae dance the swords for us the neet!*'

He runs out into the neet.

He doesn't know whether to pish himself and be sick, or be sick all down himself and pish. The indecision does for him: he's sick down himself, the hedge moves and he pishes over his leg, and as he crumples amongst the pine cones and bottles of impossible Evian, there's a liquid quack as he shits his Mammoth pants. (He can put hotels on this trio too.)

Down in the hedge Swamp Thing Tavish rests on all fours.

'Bin Laden,' he gasps, sneezing, spitting, 'I know where you're hiding, Bin Laden....' To his belly he croaks: 'Get out of there Bin Laden... stop organising tricks from inside my liver.... Go on – *shoo*....'

He splutters with laughter; once more the earth rises to his snout. He rolls on his back, but he can't see the stars. Leaves shiver far above him, blocking the chaos view.

Tavish laughs because he cannot help it.

'Hey, Bin...' he says, 'you wouldn't have an adjustable spanner I could borrow – ?'

And then suddenly he is cold. The pish has chilled on his leg, the wet shit has cooled in his pants. He is forced to move himself from the shrub.

Then he blinks into orange street-lights, the corners of his eyes moist with weariness and shame, and lopes on, thankful for the concealment of night.

'Would you?' he whispers. 'Would you?'

Drawing Apart

Isabel Adonis

Agnes was walking down the road past the Town Hall on her way to Marks when she saw him. She was with her little girl, Bonnie. She saw him crossing the road before her, smooth like he was floating over the surface of the earth: light, slender and cool, walking with a slight sway, as black boys do. A soft grey hat was balanced over soft grey, African hair, worn long in a way that she hadn't seen before: down to his shoulder almost, fluffy or nappy, the Americans say. The hat, old fashioned, in felt, with a long crease and a dark band, was sitting on the top, balanced on the mass of cotton wool hair. He was wearing sunglasses, and worn but still fairly smart corduroy trousers, old fashioned, upbeat, and a blue cotton shirt, pressed well, with a waistcoat. He had the Third Man look: rakish, distinguished, aloof, and secretive; well dressed, not only well-dressed but familiar as if she'd always known him, knew his type although he was not a type. More than that he exuded a quality that marked good upbringing. She knew that. He communicated a value she recognised and while she couldn't quite say what it was she knew that he was like her.

'There he is, Bonnie... there's that strange man again!' she said excitedly.

Agnes had seen him before, but always in the distance, slipping with that same duck-like movement, as on water, into the distance down one of the side streets or down the road to Garreg Wen. She had seen him three or four times and he was always carrying an attaché case as if he were going somewhere important.

She kept saying to herself that when she saw him again she would have to talk to him. She'd even asked complete strangers if they knew him. They always said the same thing: that they had seen him but didn't know who he was. Then, on this particular morning, he passed in front of them, across the pavement where they were walking, and onto the road. All the while he was looking, as if waiting for a sign from her, smiling as if she already knew him. It wasn't just a colour thing – the acknowledgement of like with like – but something more, going deeper inside the castle of the skin.

Agnes raised her hand and beckoned him to come over, as a queen might summon a courtier. In response, he turned and floated over to where she and Bonnie stood waiting on the pavement. She put her hand out and said hello.

'Gosh, you are cool!' she said, slightly embarrassed.

The man smiled deep. His eyes were big and dark: sexual, a bit like the wolf in the Red Riding Hood story. So sweet, too. So sweet they looked almost sinister. His eyelashes curled and looked as if they had been put on that morning. His skin was chocolate smooth like Cadbury's, whilst hers was coffee with cream. Agnes looked down at the hand holding hers. His nails were scrupulously clean and well-manicured, cut to strange points: feminine, strangers to manual work.

'I would like to write about you,' she said impulsively as he stared at her from close by. 'I just live back there by the chip shop,' she said, turning and pointing back down the road. She didn't seem to know what she was saying, which was not unusual for her. As they held hands, time stretched into a long significance.

'My name is Dr Del Mar, Dr Morris Del Mar. I was brought up in Barbados and Canada and I'm eighty years old. I flew a Lancaster bomber during the war.' Agnes remembered her mother who had had an affair with a black American pilot during the war, but said nothing.

'Wow, you look so good!' she said in surprise. 'My father was from Georgetown, in the West Indies.'

'Yes, I know,' he said, 'my brother was married to a Guyanese woman.' His voice was lilting, almost singsong. 'I am a doctor and a homeopath,' he continued, as though reciting a prepared speech. 'I have a house in Pimlico; you know, the corner of Grosvenor Road. It's worth three million. I stay in Hanover Court in Garreg Wen but it's not where I live; it's just my literary studio. I've got it all just so. It's not like the other flats. There's everything there that I need.'

'You're a writer,' she said in surprise. 'I'm a writer. I've written a novel but it's not published.'

'Is it about race... do you mention race?'

'Yes,' Agnes said. 'It's a novel about race and identity.'

'Well, that's why. It won't be published, then... no one will risk it,' he said.

'And you have a house in London?' she said in amazement, dying to know more. This wasn't just his reality; it was her dream – a house in Wales and a flat in London.

'Yes, I was there for thirty years. Now I rent the building. I kept one flat for myself. It has a plaque on the front of the building, Dr Morris Del Mar ND. FRCA.' He breathed his name as if it were full of life-giving significance. 'I go to London once a month to check up on things,' he said smiling, suave and elegant.

'Really!' She was so excited she didn't notice that Bonnie was giving her the look: the one that meant she was hanging about too much, and always with people she didn't know.

'I flew a Lancaster bomber during the war. I was in the Canadian airforce. Then I came to London,' he repeated. 'I've got a BMW; I keep it with friends. It's in the garage; I just drive it down to London. I can't drive it around here; you know what I mean.' Agnes looked at him in a questioning way. 'Black people can't be seen in expensive cars.' He was looking at her knowingly, so she quickly agreed with him, remembering once when she had been bringing back a small tree from the plant nursery, how the police stopped her and insisted on taking a cutting for analysis.

'I moved down here to write,' he said. 'I've written fifteen books; my first is already published. They follow my whole life. There's one for every five years. I've got my own publishing company, you can't trust anyone... got to do it yourself.'

'I'd like to talk to you some more,' she said enthusiastically.

'Have you e-mail?' he said.

'Yes, I'll write it for you.' She looked in her bag and saw that she didn't have a pen. 'Oh! I'm a writer with no pen,' she laughed.

'I have one,' he said, and he handed it to her.

She wrote her name: Agnes St Claire, on a piece of paper and handed it to him.

'Oh, nice name!' he said, grinning widely.

'Yes it is,' Agnes said, 'it was my grandmother's name.'

'And yours? What's your e-mail?'

He dictated an e-mail address and a website address. They didn't sound right to Agnes but she said nothing. Bonnie complained at her side and this time she noticed her daughter looking bored.

'It's time to go,' Agnes said.

'I'll phone you,' Morris said. 'I'll phone you tomorrow.' Agnes proffered her hand and he raised it to his lips. It felt strange but she tacitly agreed. Once again he looked deeply into her eyes as if willing them to fall in love. His lips were soft and large and slightly moist, his action graceful.

Agnes walked off in the direction of Marks. She felt intoxicated and intrigued.

That evening, Agnes tried to send him an e-mail, but his address didn't work, nor did his webpage. There were a few lines about him on an author's webpage but that was all. She couldn't get through on his telephone either and left him a message. She began to feel confused and sad as reality began to emerge.

'I can't get through,' she said to James.

Later that evening Morris phoned, saying he wanted to look at her manuscript the next day. He was insistent but very polite, apologising for ringing so late.

'I've left you an e-mail on the author's page. And I tried to contact you earlier by phone.'

'Oh!' he said sweetly, 'there's a light on.'

'Look I'll ring you tomorrow,' she said. 'I'll arrange to meet you somewhere.'

The next morning Agnes went out into the rain to phone by public telephone.

'Twelve o'clock at the library!' Morris said, without offering her any choice.

'OK, I'll be there... I may be a little late, but I'll be there.'

At twelve o'clock Agnes rushed to the library with her manuscript in a plastic bag under her arm. There she found two men waiting for her. They both stood as she approached the table where they sat. Morris introduced his companion; a Welsh writer called William. She took out her work and placed it on the table.

'Is this your book? I'd like to read it sometime,' William said, smiling.

Agnes was flattered but said nothing. Morris leaned forward to show her a letter from a library in Barbados thanking him for donating his book, after which he replaced it very carefully in a folder.

'Go to the desk and ask for my autobiography! It's on the shelf. They'll know where it is,' ordered Morris.

Agnes rose to her feet, hesitantly. She knew this was some kind of test but what it was, she did not know. She still felt a sense of wonder, a kind of magnetic attraction.

The librarian obediently looked on the shelf and quickly found it and Agnes returned to the desk where the two writers sat expectantly. She sat down and glanced at the blue and white front cover of what was a very thin volume, almost a pamphlet. It had been put together in a very poor way. She was immediately intrigued; drawn in, suspended again in that timeless zone. On the front of the book was a picture – like a child's drawing – in the right hand corner; a minute representation of a small boy, all black, looking through a keyhole into a bedroom where stood a four poster bed. At the end of this elegant piece of furniture was suspended the naked body of a woman, her hands tied together above her head; her face invisible. Standing directly next to her was a fully-dressed black man with a whip in his outstretched hand and in his left hand the Bible, open on a certain page. In the background was a washstand and shutter doors. She recognised the colonial setting.

Agnes felt her heart go into shock. 'A punishment,' she voiced in stony silence. She quickly looked up at Morris.

'Yes,' he said, quietly.

My picture, my punishment, Agnes thought, her feeling of fascination giving way to unease and repulsion.

She stared at the picture long and hard, her heart pounding now.

She remembered James telling her to draw a picture a few days before. She had sat down reluctantly at the dining table, cut a large piece of paper and drawn a large dressing table, shutters that had opened onto the veranda, a nondescript table that held the old Smith Corona typewriter. Grey it was, and nothing else on the table. And all the while James was watching her like it was sex or something. It was no work of art, since Agnes was never one for drawing. There were two Vono beds, government issue iron beds pushed together to make one, on a black polished floor, where her mother and father slept in an atmosphere of complete perfection, of death and unfeeling as if no person belonged there or could wish for anything.

In the foreground she drew four young girls in a row and in the background a black man holding a leather strap and a white woman at his side; the four young girls in a row all dressed identically in white T-shirts and cotton shorts, white stitching on the pockets that her mother had bought up the West End of London before they had left for Africa.

'It's a scene of confrontation,' Agnes had said as she

looked up to meet James's tender eyes, 'it's the place where I wait, speechless in dread of the punishment I never receive.'

Morris took out his fountain pen and began questioning Agnes as if he were interviewing her for a part. A role.

'How many children have you got?' he said, sickly-sweetly, almost bossy.

'Four,' she said.

'All by the same partner?'

'No,' she said. 'Three partners.'

She watched him now with suspicion as he wrote down her answers. She couldn't work out what he was doing.

William rose to his feet. 'I'm off now, I've got a few things to do.' He shook Agnes' hand, saying that he would be in touch with her.

She took out a cutting from the *Guardian* that she had in her pocket and said to Morris, 'Here's something about my dad. It's his obituary.' He seemed not to notice, although the paper was just in front of him and instead he put his hand in his bag and took out his mobile phone. He started to play with it like a small child who has been given his mother's purse to amuse himself with, no longer noticing that she was there. Agnes started to feel daft and decided that she should leave. She released what she had felt as the possibility of closeness and faced a growing isolation and despair. She rose to her feet and made some excuse about getting lunch for the girls. Morris placed her manuscript in his attaché case and shook hands with her.

As she left the library she checked out his slim volume.

Two hours later he was on the phone. 'I'm going to publish your book!' he said. 'You are not to change anything. No changes are necessary!'

'Have you read it all?' Agnes said, surprised.

'Yes. I have my own publishing arrangements. I'll get on to it straight away. It will all be done properly,' he said, 'you'll get a letter... no more messing about... my secretary will type it out. You are fifty... no point waiting... just come round to my studio with a photo. Your book will be on the shelves by Christmas.'

'I don't think I have a photo.'

'You must promise not to talk to anyone and definitely not to William.'

She agreed to see him tomorrow but by now she was feeling uncomfortable. At last someone was interested in her writing but she didn't feel happy or feel right. That lunchtime she had gone straight home to bed to read Morris' book. It was a very sad account of a boy's upbringing in the Caribbean. It spoke of terrible beatings but it was written with no feeling and no depth in a kind of fanatical, religious, analytical style. Within an hour she had read it all.

Agnes was disturbed and she needed to talk; she needed to find out some information about this man. She felt frightened although for no obvious reason and decided to contact William: he seemed pleasant enough, she thought.

'William: Morris has just phoned and he wants to publish my book.'

'Oh yes, I see.'

'I need help; I'm not sure about him. I mean, where does he live, for instance?'

'He lives in sheltered housing in Garreg Wen, you know, down by the beach.'

'Oh,' she said, surprised. 'What about his literary studio?'

'It's just a small, rather poor-looking place – there's nothing special there. One chair, I think.'

'The house in Pimlico worth three million?'

'I don't know anything about that, but if I had a house worth three million I wouldn't be living in a flat for the elderly. And if I had a Mercedes I wouldn't leave it in a garage all the while. And his book... well, he says he's printed fifteen thousand but I know he's only published two hundred. The book is full of errors and so many adjectives. Most of them he just gave away... sent them to libraries across the world. When he had his book signing at the local bookstore he only managed to sell one book and that was to a young Asian man he bullied into it. Be very cautious, that's my advice. The book says it all.'

Slowly the truth began to dawn on Agnes; she felt flat and despondent. It's all in that picture, she thought, the child drawing we both drew, and it was almost as if I expected to meet him. Then there are the stories; we both want them known. He doesn't know me and I don't know him yet in so many ways he's so much like me: the manners, the old colonial culture, the way he walks, talks. He's an odd one out too and probably has no one to talk to either. A voyeur, like me. There should be an intimacy, closeness, but there isn't. I see the pain in his eyes and he sees the pain in mine. I don't suppose either of us could admit it. Somehow there's no room for pretence with me. There's something sexual too... some unspoken sexual feeling. Agnes laughed to herself, remembering her mum saying that the reason that her sisters and her fought so much was because it was Nature's way of preventing incest.

'James, I need to get my manuscript back, but I'm frightened of something I can't say.'

'What can't you say?' James said, gently.

'I think he's going to lock the door... that somehow he can lock the door with his voice. It sounds silly, I know, but that's the way it feels.'

'I haven't met him, but you thought that this was the man who was going to make your life.'

'Yes, and he seems to want to too,' said Agnes. 'I don't know... giving up my book starts to feel like giving up my body. And I'm so scared.'

'Of a beating?' James said.

'Yes, I suppose,' said Agnes. 'It's all so weird, the meeting, the picture; him! You must come with me.'

'OK then, I'll come along,' said James. 'Have you told him?'

Agnes left a message on Morris' phone. 'The arrangement is not for me,' she said. 'I don't want you to publish my book.' Within a few minutes he rung back to say that she had to pick up the manuscript immediately as he was going away that afternoon.

Agnes and James rode down to Garreg Wen on their bikes, arriving there within a few minutes.

'I think I know where the flats are,' said Agnes. They locked up their bikes and looked for his literary studio. The flats were pleasant enough: modern, dull and institutional. They waited to hear his voice on the intercom. He opened the door and they walked up the stairs to the landing outside his flat. Agnes felt a great hollow of dread which having James with her did little to alleviate. A cheap pink carpet had been crudely laid outside his door and it looked out of place, as did the little polished table on which stood a vase of plastic flowers. On his door was a fancy brass nameplate on which was etched *Morris Del Mar*.

'This is it!' Agnes whispered to James urgently, knocking on the door. 'It's me, Agnes.'

The door opened and they entered a small, perfectly tidy room. There was a small desk in the far corner near the window, a tiny telly; one not so comfy-looking chair and what looked like an ancient answering machine. The atmosphere was dreary, tasteless – a waiting room for death, James said later.

'This is my partner, James,' she said.

'So very pleased to see you,' Morris said, as he shook hands. For a fleeting moment he seemed ashamed, exposed.

'This is my literary office,' he said, grinning like an 'umble Uriah. 'You just caught me. I was on my way to my villa in Chester for the weekend; please let me show you round,' he said, almost bowing.

He beckoned them into a minute kitchen, where there was only enough room to peer in. The next stop was a bathroom, which was a similar size, and a bedroom that didn't look as though anybody slept there. Agnes noticed a pair of leather gloves carefully placed on a side table. She felt a great sense of sorrow. Morris opened a walk-in cupboard to show them an old fashioned typewriter which looked much the same as the old Smith Corona. On it was some paper with writing half done. Agnes began to feel strange as if she had been in the room before. She recognised the feeling, the feeling which came before words.

'This is where I type my books,' Morris said proudly.

He walked over to his desk and produced her manuscript. She was surprised to see that he had already had it spiral bound with a plastic cover which he now placed in her hands. Agnes stared at the cover. She could see that by using some kind of primary school stencil and a fountain pen, Morris had created a large title, *Black Girl*, on the front. Agnes had an image of him sitting hunched up like a child, carefully outlining and filling in the spaces with his ink pen. It didn't feel like her book anymore. She felt full but there was nothing to say. The atmosphere was oppressive and sad as if they were one and the same.

'Please can I sit down,' she said and he offered her a chair.

Morris went back over to his desk and returned with a notepad.

'Here are all my ISBNs for my other books,' he said grinning to them both. 'I want three million for them; I won't accept anything less. And here's William's manuscript,' he said. It was the story of the death of his daughter, which he talked of in dismissive terms. 'I'm going to leave this for about three months before I do anything with it. I was going to do yours first because you are black.'

'What do you think about my book? You don't say,' Agnes said quietly and calmly.

He wouldn't be drawn into a discussion of her novel or his own.

'You can talk to me about anything,' he said firmly, 'but not your book.'

At this point he changed the subject and started to talk about the hall outside his room and how wonderful it was.

'Nobody else has their hallway done out like that. Do you know that the Housing people gave me this flat as a trial? They hadn't had a black person living here. I'm a pioneer. See those gardens,' said Morris pointing out of the window. Agnes rose to her feet to look at the square of green that separated the flats. It looked boring. 'They've named the garden after me!'

Agnes looked at James and said: 'It's time to go.' They all shook hands and left. The atmosphere was full of meaning, but no real words were spoken.

James and Agnes rode slowly home along the promenade. For a while they remained silent.

'I wanted to talk, James, but he wouldn't. I felt like there was so much to say, so much which held us together,' Agnes blurted out, 'But...'

'But he was in sole charge and your only rôle was submission. And you weren't going to do that.'

'No, I wasn't.'

'So there was nothing to negotiate and no communication was possible,' said James.

'It was strange... the whole thing was strange. I felt haunted by the past, like the past wasn't past.'

'He was the same age as your dad, wasn't he?'

'Yes and the same colour too,' said Agnes. 'Then there was the picture... the same picture! He personified something in me... that's what's so weird, so scary!'

Agnes remembered the image of her father. She thought of the damage to others and the damage that had probably been done to him. For the first time she felt like she could begin to understand him. The tyrant she knew was now reduced to pathos.

Every now and then, Agnes saw Morris or heard about him. Once, she met William in the street and he said that Morris was angry with her – very angry – and that he now had a new girlfriend half his age. Then one day she caught sight of him in a jeweller's shop making eyes at the young sales assistant. She stopped in the doorway for a moment and stared at him affectionately before she returned to her home behind the chip shop.

TV Land

Jon Gower

The sun might someday set over this place in tropical glory, a spaghetti of tangerine light slivers and sauvignon ribbons looped into the west. But not quite yet, not while there's more grey rain to fall. Not in this city of bad teeth, sodden litter, mangled dreams and three skyscrapers. Don't come here if you want New York's irrepressible verticality. Nor neon retina fizzes from advertising frenzy like Tokyo, nor LA chunky smog, or the sheer teemingness of Kampala. Some cities you measure in epiphanies: this one you measure with a stick.

Let's spin around the cardinal points. To the east the Great Suburbs of TV Saturation. To the north all Georgian mansions set in jungly leafiness. Old money, deep roots. To the east a garden village gone to seed and to the south, where the river used to meet the sea, they've closed the river mouth, that spastic act. You must agree.

This random city.

In a church a priest auditions new choristers with a tear of lust in his eye. They sing Bach and a piece by Arwel Hughes which conjures up pictures of snow.

A Somali boy, ten years old, recites great tracts of an oral literature passed generationally. He will learn them all, he thinks, the tales and the poems and give them to his children in turn. He is an extraordinary librarian.

In a house in Canton a man wonders how on earth he came to buy a three storey house without any stairs. There's just a big hole and a rope, thick as a naval hawser. To get to his own bathroom he has to climb like a gibbon and his hands, well they have calluses like barnacles, as if he's tried to scrape barnacles off an iron hull with his bare palms.

Three million stories like these, random and signifying.

On one street, north of the bus depot. A yellow burger van stands on a bleached out street. They are doing a roaring trade.

Marty Sathyre had a demonic smirk as he counted out the change. The punters who dined at his upmarket burger van would never guess what was really in their free range guinea fowl baguettes.

He'd been out early with the traps – set them in an avenue of decaying trees behind the bakery where collared doves and venereal town pigeons with club feet foraged and fought over the grain that slipped between lorry and silo. It took him just an hour to fill a small sack, despatching each of the birds with a Victorian police truncheon he'd boosted from an antiques market – along with a badger hair shaving brush and an ivory handled nosehair-trimmer.

Marty's Amazonian girlfriend Poppaline hated all this butchery and went on and on about it so much that Marty even thought of giving her the heave ho, were it not for her trampolining carnal skills.

His brother helped him pluck the birds and then roast them, giving them an extra ten minutes in the oven, 'just in case of disease.'

The kitchen table was sticky with gizzards and innards. Marty's hands looked like psychotic glove puppets due to the dozens of small feathers stuck there. He washed them in Swarfega, looked up the recipe for a Peruvian dish called cuy, then phoned his mate Iorwerth to line up the ingredients. Marty didn't just confine himself to cooking disease-riddled town pigeons. Oh no, his was cooking fit for an epidemiologist.

There's a popular Quechuan folk song, sung by tribes whose costume is silver suits, as if they work for NASA. Real Chariot of the Gods attire. 'Hey old lady,' goes the rhyme, 'you're as ancient as the Andes, as fickle as the wind, and if you want me as a son-in-law open the door and cook some cuy, whole cuy, mind.' And then the song turns into a call and response, 'The door, the door,' sung in a subsonic, Richard Burton voice and then the words 'the cuy, the whole one' in a castrato's falsetto, high notes like tiny bells, the singer's full spectrum.

'Iorrie, how's it hanging?'

'Could be better. Pam's left me. Said she's moving to Norwich.'

'Norwich. Jesus. Fenland. A place where a man can be his own first cousin. That is serious. So maybe I can take your mind off things. You still fit for a spot of hunting and gathering?'

'If I really have to.'

'Get me two dozen if you can.'

'Surely.'

Iorrie gathered his stuff and drove the van down to the end of the street, hung a left and pulled over. He pulled on a pair of heavy waders over his jeans, put a heavy rubber torch in his waterproof jacket, put up the portable cordon around the manhole cover, then within one move prised it open and lowered himself down.

He's got used to the smell of the sewers years ago, in fact he suspected he'd lost the sense of smell when Pam had mentioned the fragrance of night scented stock wafting out of the garden one August night and Iorrie couldn't smell a thing.

The inky water swirled and sloshed around the Victorian brickwork as he made his way to the traps. He'd bought them on the Internet, came all the way from an industrial estate in Vietnam. Best fifty quid he's spent in a long while. Best rat traps in the world and when he heard the manic squealing he knew he'd be able to fully service the order. Must be cooking cuy, he thought, as he opened the mouth of his body bag and reached down for the first to die.

A quick neck break is the best means of despatch. In Ecuador they press the small head forwards for a painless quick death and it retains the blood in the body – a big fat tick wrapped in a hairy duvet. Throat cutting is frowned upon as it leaves the meat dry, and you don't want that, now, do you?

Cuy is a pretty adaptable ingredient. Broiled or boiled. Fry one after first hammering the meat as if you mean it, exacting revenge on it, beating seven kinds of merry hell out of the flat escalopes of flesh.

Make a broth if you fancy, use snow melt from Popacatapetl and herbs only the old women in the market know about. Create a clear soup or consommé so thin it looks like dew. Taste it with a precious spoon.

Meanwhile, in one of the northern suburbs of the city a man was waking. He was Marty's nemesis, and their paths were soon to cross.

He'd known rough mornings after the night before but nothing like this. Not one where he ended up with a human foot in the sink. A bloody foot in a bloody sock in the fucking sink. Brennan stood there, transfixed by the stump, with the sheer anatomy lesson of it, the veins, the dangling tendons. He dry retched, then splashed his face with water. He had the mother of all hangovers which meant that he would have to have a high cholesterol breakfast. Food helped him think, nursed him through the occasional crisis. And this was a crisis, no doubting the stump-ended ped in his kitchen. Brennan thought there was nothing like a good pan full of fat to get him on his feet again. Kidneys. Hash browns. Cumberland sausages, plump with the wrong sort of fats. The biggest looked like a big toe. Which brought him back to the foot again. It wasn't going to simply walk away. He would have to do something about it. But not without fortifying himself with another bacon bap. He owed himself that much at least.

Where had he been the night before? He must have gone to the Green Parrot, because he always went there at the start of a bender. It was always Happy Hour down the Parrot, giveaway prices for cocktails. He'd had a Scrum Five, without the grenadine. His mother had once told him that pomegranates were the devil's own fruit so you'd do well to steer clear of them. He had, and stayed off the grenadine, which is made of pomegranates. After that he'd gone down the Meat Quarter, to goose some biff but the biff wasn't what you might call easy pickings. There'd been an octogenarian disco-queen in a PVC top, her breasts squashed like fried eggs in the strobe lights. She danced as if a surgeon had removed the part of her brain responsible for co-ordination. And there was a scar, just beneath her hairline which looked as if it was the place the neurosurgeon had tried to push some left-over matter back in.

Brennan had a few pills. He'd bought them from The Lizard, a man with skin like a crocodile handbag. Born on a toxic waste dump, that sort of complexion. There was a pink and white one and a sort of buff-coloured tablet. He took them both, not feeling in the mood for wanton experimentation. He took to the dance floor, avoiding eye contact with the go-goer, lest she ensnare him in that familiar plot which would result in a kneetrembler in the bogs. Maybe they'd been lovers once before – he couldn't remember. The DJ was transporting the dancefloor

to Ibiza. A girl was swinging her head in time to the
strobe lights, tiny droplets of sweat spraying off her hair,
an electric mist.

The pills had kicked in quick and loving warmth
coursed through the cartography of his veins. The nightclub
walls closed in on him, vectoring him back into the womb.
He felt snug in his own skin. It was during the next twelve-
inch club mix of some saccharine-laden eighties disco shite
that he passed out. Brennan has no recollection of what
happened to him. Alien abduction, maybe. The foot the
only souvenir.

When he got outside with the foot neatly wrapped and
carried in an Adidas bag Muggs was waiting for him.
Muggs worked for Luther, the head of Cardiff's mafia,
known jokingly by some as the Taffia. Brennan knew better.
Knew them to be titanium hard and bereft of scruple.

'Put your foot in it?' asked Muggs, with a breadcutter
smile.

'It's a fine day. Let's walk.'

Luther was poolside at the house with a peroxide
floozy called Tristar who'd just applied a lot of her lipstick
to his joystick. He was still flushed by his minor exertions,
fussily pulling up his trousers.

'Take a seat Mr Brennan. Can we offer you a drink?
Maybe you could do with something after last night's visit
to the horror shop.'

'I can't remember what happened...'

'We filmed it all, don't worry: the chair, the power
tools, close ups and cutaways, observed the laws of filmic
grammar.'

'Me? I did it?'

'We filmed someone who looked like you, setting about this poor man with all the righteous fury of a Jeremiah. Do you want to see?'

Brennan shook his head. The creature was there in the haze, the drug demon unleashed, the amphetamine genie run amok.

'Marty. He's the one who's brought us together. He is costing me a lot of money. My vans and shops aren't selling shit-all at the moment. And for every new van he puts on the streets I'm taking one off. Well, enough is enough. The deal is this. I want Marty's imperium to an end. Do that and your life will turn once more on a well-oiled axis, Yeats' pyre and the gyre.'

Luther was infamous for his fleet of vans, serving what the locals referred to as 'death kebabs', a choice between shish made of condemned meat and donner made of abbatoir offcuts – pigs' lips and arseholes, left over gristle, bloody floor-sweepings. Many people woke up on Sunday mornings with caves of limpid fat where their mouths used to be.

Brennan had no choice. Luther was an evil serpent, but this was a rocky path to be walked unshod. He liked Marty, respected the man's ingenuity, his naked gift of scam. And the scale of his audacity.

Like that time he sold tarmac and offered a special mix of marble which would make the owner's drive stand proud in a long street of driveways. It would cost a bit more, mind, he would caution with that way of his of establishing a truth-teller's eye contact. After they'd laid it, the effect of the white chips – 'from a family-run quarry outside Turin' against the jet black of the mac was striking. He'd shake hands, they'd pack the lorry and, come the first rain, the Polo mints they'd thrown in the mix would melt and the drive would become a pockmarked mess.

Or the bootlegging. Marty captured some of the all-time best gigs on his miniature recording equipment, made on the sly by his cousin Wilf who worked in a hush hush MOD lab somewhere near Aberdeen. He was the first to release Brian Wilson's *Smile*, that work of dark symphonic majesty which, had it come out before the Beatles' *Sergeant Pepper*, would have made the Fab Four look like the Muppets they really were.

Two months flew by at an amphetamine lick as Brennan made his plans.

Meanwhile Marty's success bred more success. He bought fifteen more vans with a grant from the Welsh Development Agency – scamsters themselves in shiny suits. He had the coolest of logos designed by Pete Fowler, the guy who does the Super Furry Animals' artwork. It was a dining dragon, the creature resplendent in a white tuxedo and quite the apogée of monster sophistication. And over a round of Warsteiners in Chapter bar his friends brain-stormed a logo for him.

'Enter the Dragon.'

'Too Chinese.'

'Or perverse.'

'What about Marty's Mess, like they have on ships?'

'Too messy.'

'Or Perfect Taste.'

'I like that.'

And so was born the slogan that would wrap around the base of the dragon's tail.

Demand threatened to outstrip supply. Fast food normally commands a fat profit margin but the four hundred per cent mark-up at PT's made the usual look anorexic. It made it worth creating a small team who would trap underground and venture up the valleys to catch pigeons. They paid a farmer called Steve a lavish retainer for keeping quiet and laying out corn in stubble fields where they would use rocket-powered nets which could capture a flock at a time.

The menu expanded:

Perfect Taste
Grilled spatchcock burgers (collared doves collared behind the bakery – same weight as a spatchcock only a damn sight cheaper) £4.00
Guinea fowl with grape baps (woodpigeons by another name) £3.50
Wild rabbit with organic green leaf (sewer kill mainly and kids were paid by the carrier bag to collect dandelions) £4.50

They sited the vans near office blocks at lunch time, drove to events, even went to agricultural events where no one so much as asked a question. Lips were smacked. Taste buds were tantalised. They raked it in off the vans. One made eight grand in five days. There was a bad incident one night when a bunch of yobs overturned a van which caught fire and the man inside, Terry Fetch, only just managed to clamber out with his life, through the hatch. He was lit up like a magnesium flare, his clothes burning into his dermis and he screamed like a wild banshee. The only yob who hadn't legged it rolled the flames out with a coat and then scarpered. Marty paid for the plastic surgery, jokingly offering to make him look like Robbie Williams but Terry never smiled after that night, wasn't able to, really, not with the way they had to reconfigure his jaw. That was the only shadow on what seemed like a perfectly sunlit summer.

It was an October afternoon when a television researcher rang Marty to ask him whether he'd like to be a guest on the Johnnie Smooth chat show. Marty said yes, with alacrity. He'd never been on tv and he liked Johnnie Smooth, his ready banter and punishing asides. 'You're as welcome as syph' was one of his catchphrases, this self-crowned 'King of the Putdown'.

The velveteen-voiced honey ended the chat with Marty: 'Next Thursday, live on air at seven, so you'll need to be at the studio by half past five if that's all right, for some make-up and a quick run through. We'll send a cab for you – to the house, yes?'

'I look forward to it, Melissa.'

Melissa who was on Brennan's payroll now. As was Johnnie, although his help came because of morality rather than money, convinced by Brennan that what he was about to do was for the public good.

The make-up lady was a doll and the researcher, Melissa, was a doll and the producer of the programme, Henry, was a gushing London queen slumming it in regional television after an accident during the making of a documentary at the British Museum when he'd insisted on getting a better angle on a Ming vase which he nudged off the table. The crew and the mortified curator seemed to count the minutes before it hit the floor, smithereening itself out of history.

'May I say,' simpered Henry who would have made a good Beatrice or Delilah, tottering on heels, 'that I think your burgers are ravishing. Quite the best this side of the Atlantic and you could even give them a run for their money Stateside. Ever thought of franchising over there?'

Marty hadn't until Henry put up the idea and he squirrelled it away. He knew that people lived in the sewers in New York, which might be an advantage, maybe not and he knew that they'd hunted down the passenger pigeon – once the most numerous bird on earth, flocks darkening the sun – until there was just one left, shuffling off a perch in San Diego zoo, a ten-inch drop to extinction.

'Let's take you to meet the man,' said Henry.

They went through a labyrinth of corridors until they reached a door marked with an enormous star, with dozens of thin strips of gold fanning out from its centre.

They knocked and entered.

'Come in! Come in! Care for a blueberry margarita? Heaps of vitamin C. Let me tell you, Marty, I do admire your products. Very much.'

'Have you ever tried any?' ventured Marty with a certain bitterness. His hackles were up because Johnnie addressed him via the mirror, not deigning to turn around.

'My researcher brought in a wild leveret thing which

tasted pretty divine. You've got some good product and I
hear Mammon's looking after you well?'

'Mammon?'

'The God.'

'I know who Mammon is but what are you trying to
imply?'

'Nothing, chum. Look, don't get in a tizz. Don't get my
stage persona mixed up with the fifty-two-year-old bloke
who's been on the rollercoaster. I've seen ups and I've seen
downs and at the moment I'm having a drink to settle my
nerves before delivering verbal bad ju-ju to the nation. Why
don't you? People get nervous under the television lights.
We had to give one contributor, a taxidermist from
Prestatyn, a cup of tea laced with Mogadon before we
could get him on the set. Trouble was he'd had a few slugs
from a hip flask apparently and we only just managed to
stop him attempting fake coitus with a stuffed leopard he'd
brought in. On air, mind! In front of all those people.'

'I'll have what you're having.'

'And if we're talking about gods,' said Johnnie, 'these
are their faces.' He pointed to what seemed like a mini-
shrine in the corner, a four foot high block of cork to which
were attached a collection of men's faces.

'These are the tabloid men, the ones who make
and break people like me. *Daily Star*, *Mirror* and most
pungently, the *Sun*. And here's my favourite headline
from that august organ. The Institute for Strategic Studies
wanted a pacifist, a token pacifist to join their board and
they invited Michael Foot because he was just about the
most famous one around at the time – even though Bruce

Kent was probably the pacifists' pacifist – and he accepted. The *Sun* ran it under the headline 'Foot Heads Arms Body'. Marty was laughing as he sipped his powerful margarita.

In the technical area the floor manager was saying his mantras, learned from a wise man in a tree-house in Kerala.

'The water lapping the mangrove roots is the sound of a safe place, is the rhythm of home.'

He took a deep breath and walked into studio D to do the warm-up routine, the usual limp-as-lettuce gags followed by the health and safety drill. On air in ten.

The director in the gallery looked at his watch. Almost an hour before he could get to a bar and shaft a lager and maybe if his luck was in, pull one of the impressionable little vixens who worked in accounts. The production assistant sitting next to him was wondering if the small wager she'd had with Camera 4 would pay off. She'd predicted that tonight was the night Johnnie's show would drop off the ratings graph. This run had been getting worse and worse and they simply weren't getting the names and in this celebrity age that was the kiss of death. And talking to a guy who flipped burgers for a living wasn't exactly Big Brother in Buck House now, was it?'

Melissa had told her this show might be better than she could imagine. Precocious bitch. All that Oxbridge la-dee-dah!!

The audience was a blue rinse brigade from some Women's Institute up the valleys, who found Johnnie as shocking as the advent of menopause. It was always some Women's Institute from up the valleys who arrived in buses that had seen better days and those were the days of GI

brides and ration books. There was also the younger crowd
who liked the scabrous humour of mine host.

The resident band, with its vertically-challenged
musical director Billy Sharp struck up the familiar tune,
marred somewhat by the fact that the trumpeter coughed
during the middle eight and made a sound like some
German sound terrorists.

The floor manager counted down and in he walked
– down the glass stairs with the fur-lined bannisters in a
zebra striped suit with pink chunky-heeled winkle-pickers
and did that mince of his that made him a gay icon to rival
the Beverley Sisters, all of them. The biddies hooted and
hollered, the youngsters bayed in appreciation, the sounds
of calving elephant seals, an uproar of applause.

'Glamorous people, a good night and the warmest of
welcomes to the show of shows. And if your name happens
to be Graham Norton – go pinch other people's ideas, you
bag of spent fuck.'

The audience went off like a firecracker, fake shock
and real shock. For the tv audience the expletives would be
bleeped out by a nimble-fingered vision mixer. It was all a
part of living on the edge.

A crash of snare drums. Marty appeared in a backlit
window to the side of the stairs. He forced a smile through
his mask of pinking embarassment.

'And we have for you a self-made man, a man of
means, not a mean man. His name is Marty Sathyre and
he's the King Farouk of fast food, the top cat of takeaway
and a genuine burgher of this town. More from him later,
but we start – where, Billy? Spinning round to where his

MD was just climbing down from his conductor's wooden box.

'I don't fucking know, ya knobhead.'

'So what have you got there. What are you eating on the sly?'

'Shortbread.'

The audience went off on one. They loved the predictability of the dwarf jokes – the shortarse slot as some called it. He dismissed Billy with a hand gesture and looked at Camera 3.

'Who wants to come up here and try their luck with Johnnie?'

Three quarters of the audience had their hands up, but tonight they weren't choosing at random. Dirk was a plant, there to add spice to Marty's night of tv hell.

The steadicam operator tracked him from his seat to his place in front of Johnnie's throne.

'And you are?'

'Dirk.'

'So nothing normal there. You are the chosen one, the lucky bottom feeder chosen from the pond life that is tonight's studio audience. Now kneel and kiss my pickers.'

Dirk did as he was told. Week on week they all did. After all there was a holiday in Rio resting on the next minute.

'What do you do when you're not feeding on the bottom, or maybe it's some man's bottom. *Ych a fi*, what an image. I'll need electroshock to expunge that image out of my head: you parting a pair of clenchies with your horrible fat tongue.'

Dirk stood up.

'So what do you do, Dirk?'

'I'm a-a-a-trading standards officer.'

'A s-s-s-tammering standard trading officer.'

'No, it's trading...'

'I know what it is, you smeg-brained fucking yokel. Hit that button, Meg, keep us on air, why don't you?' Meg would resign after tonight. It was ridiculous what she had to go through, what with the Head of Programmes saying it would be her fault if any Anglo-Saxon swearing made it into Welsh TV Land.

'What do you do exactly?'

'I'm working on some food fraud.'

'Would that be fast food coz if it is you might like to meet my main guest. Stick around for him.'

The light came up behind Marty's head but this time he looked quizzical, a tremor of nerves animating his lower lip so that he looked as if he was on the verge of saying something.

'Anyway let's see what the viewer's choice is tonight.' (Viewers were invited to send things in for the contestants to taste, blindfold. They were encouraged to send in either something too vile for words or something nice, Samaritan food.)

'Let's see, we've got a mouth-watering selection of Vomitorium Surprise, Preparation X and Aztec Two Step, each served on doilies hand-made by some of the darling ladies of the audience.'

The camera tracked along the third row, where the gleeful ladies were having the times of their lives even as

Johnnie invited them to join in the chant.

'Choose, choose!'

Dirk's finger hovered over Preparation X (sent in by Mrs D Roberts of Blaenau Ffestiniog, an apprentice witch of the high slate country). He then pointed at the Aztec Two Step.

'Knife and fork for Dirk, not that you need a knife, seeing as a dirk is a small Scottish knife. That would suit you Billy, wouldn't it – a short Scottish knife, you fucking stupid dwarf.' Meg the vision mixer missed that one: there were ructions.

Two scantily-clad leggy blondes tottered in on high heels, one bearing a fork and another bearing a knife. Expect the death threats from the feminists, thought Henry.

Dirk ate the food, which after the first moment of imagined revulsion caused no revulsion. In fact it tasted very pleasant.

'What d'ya think, Dirk, darling?'

'V-v-very nice.'

'Is it indeed, Dirk – well we'll find out later what it is you've allowed into your alimentary. Let Kylie and Charlene take you over there to sit down so you can digest things. Dirk, ladies and gentlemen! What a waste of a skin!'

The band played the sting that announced the evening's main guest.

The assistant floor manager ushered him onto the staircase and he was momentarily dazzled by the lights: a small deer caught in the headlights of a rumbling Mack truck.

He sat down in the chair opposite Johnnie, a seat deliberately upholstered to allow the guest to sink in and look uncomfortable right from the outset.

'Well, Marty. They tell me you're a millionaire, not that you could tell from your clothes.'

'Wah-wah,' went the trumpet, applauding the joke.

'As I said you're a self-made man. Who made you – Baron Frankenstein?'

Even though Marty was not bad looking, he seemed uglier, slumped into the sofa, which managed to make him look winded. He also hadn't managed to get a word in yet.

'You've created a small empire of burger vans – top class stuff, haven't you?'

'Yes,' managed the discomfited Marty, who was starting to sweat now. He was aware of a droplet gathering on the tip of his nose.

'So where do you get the recipes from – do you steal them from books or are you an inspired chef?'

'I've picked them up on my travels.'

'My, my. This is an educated fellow we behold. Articulate. Loquacious and erudite as evidenced by those well-chosen words. And where has our well-travelled wordsmith peregrinated in this fair planet?'

'I've been here and there.'

The audience squealed at his embarrassment.

'Ever been to Latin America, Marty – ever ventured there? They eat guinea pigs down there, I hear.'

Camera 4 cuts to Dirk's face, alert now to evidence.

Marty is caught in a Trappist silence.

'Do you know what would be a wicked wheeze, with

the emphasis on wicked. What if you substituted sewer rats, good old rattus norvegicus for guinea pigs and served those up on a bap. That would make good business sense, wouldn't it? Tell me now, wouldn't it?'

Marty tried to get up but the sofa restrained him.

'Ladies and gentlemen. This man, Marty Sathyre, does precisely that – serves up rats in burgers, pigeons in kebabs, all manner of unspeakable filth and has the audacity to dress it up as fine provender. Let's bring on Dr Filigree Watson, an expert on animal pathology.'

A pantomime mad scientist makes his entrance, an eggshell-head above the obligatory bow tie.

'You've examined the contents of Mr Sathyre's products, Dr Watson. What do you deduce?'

'I have no doubt that the main ingredients on the menu of Perfect Taste include the brown rat, the common wood pigeon, collared doves and some evidence of crow and grey squirrel.'

'But they're not described as such on the menus, are they Marty?'

'No they're not.' And with those words his number was well and truly up. On cue from the floor manager, Kylie and Charlene wheeled the familiar wooden contraption into place in front of the band area where its members were donning sou'westers and rubber coats.

The audience broke into spontaneous braying.

'The stocks! The stocks.'

Zombified by shame, Marty was led to the stocks where his hands were slotted through the holes and one by one, in a curiously sombre Indian file, the audience members walked up, row by row, to hurl buckets of food swill at him. Not a frenzy: all designed to ensure that he was still being drenched as the credits rolled. They intercut shots of Dirk being sick in a huge brown bag.

In a house on the southern rim of the city a priest was watching the box to fill his mind after what had happened after choir practice – another young life besmirched – like wiping an oily rag across an innocent cheek.

Even though warned about the deadening effect of television, a very young Somali has rested awhile from his feats of memory, to watch the buckets being hurled, embarrassed that his grasp of English wasn't sufficient to understand all of Johnnie's badinage.

In a house in Canton a man switched off the set and went to piss in a bucket coz he didn't have the energy to climb the rope to the bathroom.

As the announcer's voice went into the 'same time next week' spiel, Luther opened a bottle of Cristal champagne and punched in the numbers of Brennan's mobile so he could congratulate him for a job well done. His girlfriend Tristar cut a couple of lines of coke, her long, black-painted fingernails clacking on the mirror surface like crows' beaks. The Bolivian marching powder was high grade. It would be a night of manacles and sweat.

In his dressing room the star of the show took off his jacket and put it carefully on a hanger. He thought to himself about the wares he peddled, which pulled people together, brought them close. This virtual community in a world going mad. This flickering lamp, lighting the faces of the brain-dead, who'll go on watching even as the stars descend and the cities burn. Watch it in widescreen, watch it on plasma screen. Watch it any which way. Johnnie knows.

Changes

Huw Lawrence

Rebecca was sitting on the sofa, twig-like, smoking a joint. The Pink Floyd was on the stereo. She was fond of things that belonged to the past, for example, clothes. She was sewing some frilly, period-looking garment, needles sticking out of the arm of the sofa.

At twenty-six she was older than I, but not older than my girlfriend, Nia, who was a staff nurse. Rebecca received a fair amount of cash from her long-suffering father but was wasteful and so lived under the same cheap roof as us. A year ago she'd had her nose done. She was sleeping with one of her lecturers and had a therapist.

'I'm glad you decided to come up,' she said, 'I want to talk.'

'OK. Talk.'

'Alistair called. He wants me to pay something towards

the mortgage on the flat. Also he wants me to go back to him. He's begging me.'

'So, what's new, Bec?'

'What shall I do?'

'What does your therapist say?'

'I'm not seeing him till Tuesday.'

'The Social Security pays the mortgage,' I pointed out.

'You think he's a prick, don't you. You think they're all pricks. The only one you don't think is a prick is Jawad.'

I didn't answer.

Jawad was purposeful, bent on success, a foreign student who virtually lived in the library. Like Rebecca, he studied psychology. He was amazingly poor. His room, scarcely larger than a road-mender's hut, displayed photographs of his family. Rebecca was not a good student. She put in little effort and her essays were always late. Jawad helped her, spending the occasional night with classy Rebecca.

'What can I do if only pricks fancy me?' she said, in a lonely voice, from which I deduced that one evening soon I'd see her in high heels and make-up, going out, tall and glossy as a new nail, to pull someone new for a change.

Rebecca was concerned about the existence of the 'self', meaning her own. She wasn't anxious to develop it so much as to be sure it was there, able to add up to something one day. 'Just continuing isn't enough,' she'd insist. 'We're not just programmes. We're not just data.' She would tap her head, quaintly. 'I'm in there.'

Yet the only consistent thing about her was the packet of sherbet lemons she always carried in her handbag.

'You're asking the wrong one for advice on Alistair,' I said.

She knew that my mind was on a career above all else, not marriage, and certainly not her marriage.

I'd grown up in a town that turned into a catastrophe overnight. Shops were boarded up and houses had concrete blocks for windows, teaching you what money enabled you to avoid. The government might still have bribed the Japs to open a factory. There'd been talk. But there was as much chance of revitalising the place as of me winning the Lottery.

I'd settle for a job with prospects.

Anywhere.

You'd have thought Nia, who came from another valley where the same was true, would have understood this better than Rebecca, whose home had its own tennis courts. But Nia had dissimilar views from me on everything. Nia lived for the day and said home was where the heart was, but what kind of home was it that everyone left? She'd left. My mother wanted to leave now my father had died. I'm remorseless, as single-minded as Jawad, who'll try his best not to go home to Pakistan, which is even poorer than my home.

'Don't you have any female friends to ask,' I enquired, 'who might have views on marriage?'

'Poor Nia,' Rebecca said, inconsequentially.

'Why?'

'Well, doesn't she love you, poor girl?'

'Don't you have any girl friends?' I repeated.

'I tried it,' she said, 'but I prefer men.'

I was fond of her. I loved Nia but I was fonder of Rebecca. She asked for little, if asking for a sense of your own reality is little. It isn't, I suppose, if you haven't got it. How her father came by such a daughter, I can't imagine, because he was a man of firm beliefs. I suppose Rebecca found they didn't apply. Yet Rebecca was supportive of a man's principles, while stretching them to the limit, hoping they'd break. When not unloosening her life story, she didn't talk much, content to be the world's most dangerous listener. She remembered everything you said.

I told her that she collected lovers because she needed to store up approval, and her long face with its slender, beautiful nose nodded encouragement. She was fond of analysis, emotions, confessions. She had expressions and gestures just for the occasion. She had a special voice that mixed anguish and desire like vinegar and honey in her throat. All she really wanted from her lovers was a devoted ear and some small gift of bric-a-brac that would represent them in the endless story of herself.

Some, like Jawad, with more pressing things on their minds, didn't mind sharing her, and continued to make small gifts, symbolically adding to themselves. However, most lovers were hurt to discover they were just one of a number. They crept away, pining, but remained her friends, unable to hate someone who'd made them part of her life.

Heartless Rebecca!

'I don't think I have the right attitude, or conversation, or something — with women, I mean,' she said, giving my question her consideration. 'No, I don't seem to have any women friends.'

Her skirt rose a fraction and her legs opened a little as she made herself more comfortable on the sofa. She laughed at nothing. It sounded like a bell in a waiting room.

She tossed her long black hair away from her face and drank very slowly from a glass of orange juice, as if it were a potion from a sympathetic witch who had distilled the meaning of life. She shook her head to recollect herself, sending her hair awry, and offered me the joint. I declined.

In the room was a trunk that had slept under bric-a-brac since arriving. The sideboard had bric-a-brac, too. She had a small, antique teddy bear that wore a dress and smelled of camphor. Or had I imagined it?

'Didn't you have a teddy bear?' I asked.

'It's in the sideboard,' she said.

In the corner of the room, in shadow, a tall plant with waxy leaves turned up the palms of its many hands. I wouldn't have wanted to get stoned with that for company.

She raised her eyes to mine: huge, deep eyes. A line of mysterious poetry wrote itself on her forehead.

'Why,' she asked, 'do you want me to have female friends all of a sudden?' Her voice was husky. 'Is it because most girls do? Is it because you think it's normal?' She spoke the word 'normal' as if it were a food eaten by the very poor, then grinned, wickedly, as if abnormality were more desirable.

'Probably,' I said.

'You're like an igloo,' she sighed, shifting accommodatingly on the sofa, 'and you don't let anyone in to warm you up.'

Did she recognise in me something of her own problem?

I had inquired once what advice her sixty-year-old therapist gave her. She told me he just listened.

The things you can get on the National Health!

Her black eyes opened very wide. Her skirt was even higher than before. Her wide mouth smiled as she talked.

'You're not ready to get involved with anyone seriously. You said so yourself, remember?'

I shrugged.

She ran the tip of her tongue wickedly along the rim of her upper lip. Her face pleaded, child-like, then became destitute, and then mock solemn to mimic mine. Finally, she gave this up, emitting a wild, outcast laugh she'd perfected, an unhinged soprano alarm meant to elicit concern. I told her she sounded like a canary on acid.

'I'm not offended,' she said, humbly.

Then she asked: 'Do you write about me in your diary?'

'It's just a notebook,' I said.

'Am I in it?'

'Not in the way you think.'

It was probably a lie, but I didn't want to discuss my diary. It was a bit like her life story, an unsure contrivance which made others into what I wanted them to be.

'Come and sit by me, and tell me about it,' she said, patting the sofa beside her.

'Time to make coffee,' I said.

I made for the kitchen.

Her coffee was always worth having.

Her father was in the coffee business and it arrived regularly through the post in brown paper parcels. He was a small, awkward man with a questioning manner, always smartly dressed in a suit. His name was Joe, Joe Wise. He once had a partner called Solomon, making the business Solomon and Wise.

'The respect for quality is going,' he said to me, once, standing in that same kitchen. 'Everything's equal today.'

He wasn't talking about coffee. I never heard him talk about coffee.

'Eequality, that is; Mr Wise,' I joked, straight-faced.

'Very good, Gavin,' he retorted, dryly.

After all his years in this country his accent was still foreign and thick, though he spoke English perfectly. He'd been got out of Poland as a child, to escape the concentration camps, yet over all the years the inflections of English had not rubbed off on him.

'If there isn't any better or worse, what's the point in doing anything difficult?' he asked.

'Everything's either too easy or impossible these days,' I replied.

He granted me this with a typically Jewish gesture of his hand.

Then he told me a joke, cracked by Isaiah Berlin to a philosopher acquaintance, he claimed, as they passed two women quarrelling from their respective doorsteps – 'arguing from different premises.'

I laughed, politely.

'Did you know,' he said, 'in ancient Greece people

having trouble with their emotions went to see a philosopher? You would have had paid employment, Gavin.' He slapped me on the shoulder affectionately, emitting a series of guttural chuckles.

'I made a bad choice of subject,' I conceded. 'If I could get enough teaching hours at the college I'd save up and do a conversion course, part-time.'

'What to?' he asked.

'Law,' I replied.

'Pah!'

When he visited his daughter in her student surroundings he liked to recount two occasions when he found himself caught up in riots: in Athens and Paris. From him I heard about the Greek Colonels and Papandreos, Danny the Red, The Angry Brigade, The Red Brigade, Bader Meinhof.... He'd made himself an expert, first on those two particular riots and then on the whole period. Being in the wrong place twice had turned him into quite an historian.

'Why not history, Gavin?' he suggested. 'A better companion for your philosophical studies.'

'It would give me no more chance of a job.'

'Is that the most important thing?'

'It is when you haven't got one.'

He sighed. 'People used to believe in things, you know, Gavin. People wanted to improve society.'

'I don't dare think about society, I've got attitude appraisals to worry about,' I joked.

I must have sounded less flippant than I thought.

'What a pity, Gavin,' he said.

I shrugged.

'What's society, Mr Wise? These days they even dispute the existence of history.'

He was silent, and I was sorry I'd said that.

'But I believe in history, Mr Wise,' I added. 'And I believe people should learn from it.'

He smiled, sadly.

'You're a good boy at heart, Gavin,' he said.

He sniffed the air above his long, hooked nose as if he hoped it might contain some nourishment.

Then he said: 'God bless my soul.'

I returned from the kitchen and put Rebecca's coffee down beside her.

She had put away her sewing. She put her hand on my wrist. 'Do we have to wait till someone else dies before we can make love?' she asked, sad and insistent. 'Gavin?' she pleaded, like a hurt little girl, pursing her lips for a kiss.

How could she make herself look so vulnerable?

I gave her a peck and returned to my chair to drink my coffee. She gave an elaborate shrug.

The last time we'd slept together we'd both been touched by the sudden death of a stranger after coming upon a road accident. It hadn't been a particularly horrible sight, but we were shocked.

My own parents understood, of course, but it was Joe Wise who found words: 'Let it remind you of all that unites you with the living.'

I wrote that in my diary.

I wrote down a number of the things he said. In that year's diary I have a small portrait of a man who talked as though life had a meaning beyond his own existence.

'Why won't you make love to me? Why must it be just that once?' flared Rebecca.

She was indignant, quite uninfluenced by the fact that Nia, on early morning shift, was asleep downstairs.

'Why withhold yourself? What's the point?'

What, indeed? I wondered.

I sighed the sigh of someone wanting more than just a job. I heard that sigh. I heard in it someone wanting a future with some point to it.

'Nia must be able to trust me,' I replied.

'Why?'

That accident: Rebecca had left her handbag at her favourite lecturer's house, his wife being away, and I'd gone along for the ride when she'd driven back out for it. He was a slim, agile guy of about forty, full of exhausting charm and unaware I knew of their affair. He'd talked to Rebecca about her work and given us coffee and cashew-nut biscuits.

Then we'd driven back into town. It was dusk.

We were the first on the scene.

Straight away Rebecca called 999 on her mobile. The doors were too buckled to open. An elderly stranger in a mackintosh with silver hair on either side of his hat stared blindly at us through the windscreen. He vaguely resembled my father in appearance. He swayed to and fro alarmingly as the firemen wrenched open the door with a crowbar. We felt so relieved when he was found to be alive. Later, when we telephoned the hospital, we learned he'd died in the ambulance.

Feeling futile and strangely heartless we'd drunk wine and smoked a couple of joints, harking back disbelievingly to the swaying, seated victim, to whom death had come as such a surprise, and who had made me think of my father. Then we'd gone to bed and made love, because we were alive, because we needed to take our minds off what there were no words for.

When she spoke next Rebecca's voice was dreamy.

'The garden is all moonlight,' she sighed.

She'd given up her proposal. She'd forgotten her question. God knows what was in her head by then. I doubt it was her life story.

'There used to be too many greens for just one word,' she said, sadly, 'but they all look grey now.'

'What greens?' I said. 'It's autumn.'

Later, near the end of that year, when Joe Wise died I ended up in bed with Rebecca again, while Nia worked a night shift. He died of a heart attack, like my own father, dead-heading roses in a friend's garden. I held Rebecca tight, grieving for both fathers, weeping and intermittently having sex, which made no more sense than dying, but took our minds off it.

I still have that diary from 1992.

We can't afford to give up. We have to trust each other, even criminals and lunatics.

When our humanity doesn't recognise itself in others, we

won't know why we are alive anymore.

Sometimes, feeling lonely or lost, Joe Wise's face would come to mind, sadder than anything his daughter could imitate, and yet he was a man who went on believing in others, despite everything. And sometimes I'd try to cheer myself up by imagining him in one of his fine suits, discovering that his daughter had brought an unexpected new nose into the family and that one they had loved for centuries had vanished.

Alexandra Claire

Playing The Odds

A structure floated in space. All around it was night. There were no stars, but the Earth was anchored nearby as a point of reference.

The body was spherical with no outer shell. It was entirely made up of rooms, each having one door but no stairways or visible access to other levels.

She understood the game. There were no rules. There were no patterns. Intellect was impotent. Here, everything ran by chance. Her life was at stake.

She moved from room to room from the bottom level towards the upper level. Sometimes this signified progression, sometimes regression. The result of her action was only known to her when each decision she made had been executed. The knowledge gained was immediately lost as it meant nothing and gave her no power. She began to move by instinct and without consideration.

Time ran fast forward and stood still. She understood that time did have significance but it was untenable, so she moved on. Someone tried to speak to her but before she could exhale, her attention was drawn over her shoulder by a figure dressed in white. As the figure passed through a doorway, Seren evolved into the final chamber. The annoyance of the person trying to speak to her had split him into two identical beings. She had also split, but one part had no weight and left with the spirit.

Again he tried to speak to her. As he did so, she became aware of the spirit and her own, weightless self leaving. Their force was pulling Seren with them, through the doorway and out of the structure. His cold breath trickled down her neck. His words pressed into her ear: 'And next time, I'll kill you.'

Lost in that strange, disordered place between sleep and wakefulness, eventually adrenalin pushed her over into consciousness. It was an uneasy passage and only fear stopped her slipping back. Her eyelids were heavy and she fought to keep them open. She tried to pull into focus the objects in the room. The chest of drawers. The window, where she registered the texture of matter meeting the pulse of the streetlight. As soon as her fear had subsided enough, she slipped back into the darkness of sleep and lost herself.

She never did quite find herself again. Part of her consciousness, part of her self was lost to the ether.

Alexandra Claire

Los Pajaritos, Seville

Seren's fingers drummed away on the table. The sunshine outside enticed and oppressed her at the same time. He wouldn't take long in the shower. Thank God, she hadn't had to listen to his toilet sounds. That would have been too much for her. She came from a very private family, who never went to the toilet.

Seduced from her chair, she walked across the room to the tiny window. The tiled floor was deliciously cool to the soles of her feet. She stuck her head and shoulders out of the window and her cheeks were immediately singed by the ridiculous heat. She thought that this was how it might feel to stick her head in the oven: not unbearable. 'Resumé' by Dorothy Parker came to mind and her eyes lit up. The cynicism comforted her enormously.

In the block immediately opposite, windows were wide open. She glimpsed snatches of other peoples' lives. In one flat, the walls were painted the same blue as her grandmother's sitting room in Surrey. There were dark oil paintings in ornate, heavy gilt frames. Occasionally, the torso of a well-built man, wearing a white vest, would join the paintings. The torso smoked heavily and seemed upset. He remonstrated passionately with someone but no other torso joined him in the window. Her eyes shifted to other windows. Many of them had caged songbirds on their ledges. It seemed cruel somehow, to put a bird in a cage out of doors. Less colourful wild birds cascaded by and taunted the jailbirds with their flight. The earth floor of the yard between the two blocks of flats had dried and compacted through time and drought. The earth was the same colour as rich sand. A crumpled, smiling widow cut through the yard on her way home from the fish market. Her heels antagonised the earth and dust rose in her wake.

Jaime came out of the bathroom and went into his bedroom to dress. She had the feeling that he had wanted her to turn from the window and look at him, to acknowledge his movements in some way. This unsettled her and even though it wasn't yet midday, she went to the fridge to get herself a beer.

The fridge was crammed with whole Manchego cheeses and chorizos, multi-packs of this and that. Jaime lived alone and rarely entertained, yet he always bought in bulk. He had told her that this was because he hated shopping. She suspected him of being a miser. Her eyes felt uncomfortable in their sockets. He seemed to habitually agonise over the most mundane decision, always citing the cheapest option. He would glance at her, one questioning eyebrow raised, anxious that her wants and needs would not exceed his price limit. She poured the cold, gold beer into a glass. At home she would have drunk from the can. Here, for some reason, she needed to feel civilised. There was a jade velvet sofa next to the window. It was softly and seductively shaped. Apart from some flimsy folding chairs, it was the only thing to sit on. Despite this, neither of them ever did sit there. The sofa had no give. It was unco-operative. His father had made it by hand. Jaime often enthused to friends about his beautiful, hand-stitched sofa.

When he came out of his bedroom, she was standing

barefoot in the middle of the room, sipping her beer and looking at the window. He wrapped his arms around her waist and squeezed. She was looking at the air conditioning system fixed onto the outside wall of the torso's flat. It was cool enough to argue within those blue walls.

'Shall we eat here darling, before we go out? It will be cheaper you know.' He glanced at her, raising one, questioning eyebrow. Seren laughed, a little.

El Rocio

They reached a compromise over the food and made a picnic of bread, olives, jamon, tomatoes and Cruzcampo. He was glad because it was cheap. She was glad because it was unusual.

Seren felt guilty about her uncharitable thoughts towards Jaime, so she put on a cobalt silk dress that she knew he particularly liked. Damn it, if she was honest with herself, she wore it because she got a kick out of being admired by him. As they were leaving, Jaime remembered to pick up the kitchen rubbish. He handed the bag to Seren.

'You take this to the bin. I'll take the other bags and meet you at the car; I need to check my mailbox.'

The pungent bag swung in her hand as she ran down the stairs and out into the courtyard. There was a council workers' strike on in Seville and the rubbish hadn't been cleared from Los Pajaritos for a week. The strike had coincided with a particularly hot June. Mounds of decomposing waste spilled out of the community bins, rampaged into the streets and violated the air. The secret, repellent vestiges of local life, cooked for days in the fierce sun, liquefied and leaked from plastic bags. Just yards from the decay, in a haze of heat and odour, two men sat in the shade playing cards. They paused from their game and watched as Seren passed by. She could feel their eyes attempt to seep through the outer layer of her skin. She looked down and retaliated, through will alone, and defended every pore. Whilst locked in battle, words chalked on the pavement in front of, then under, then behind her feet read: 'And next time, I'll kill you.'

A flash flood of adrenalin, sensual shutdown and she focused calmly and completely on the task in hand. The bag was hurled up into the air and Seren paid meticulous attention as debris joined debris and the waste-mound shook to greet the latest member of its rejected, unclaimed body.

She tore her eyes away and ran to the car. Jaime put the cool-bags and beach paraphernalia onto the back seat and covered them with a torn sun visor. They slammed the doors, he turned on the ignition and they escaped the heat of Seville.

The route they took out of the city was fast, four-laned and walled in by two-storey cubes of shops and distribution centres. The facades of metal and glass were opaque with years of exhaust fumes, pumped out by vehicles speeding into the heart of the city or out to the cool of the coast. The road was just like any other road, out of any other city in Europe. Seren had been introduced to

Seville along this road and she now knew that it bitterly belied the beat, fire and rhythm at its source.

They drove south towards Matalascanas. The ever-increasing miles between Seren and Los Pajaritos eased the tension in her contracting mind. She began to slowly massage her temples, winding threads of warm, salty, wet hair around her fingers, then she leaned towards the open window and surrendered to the breeze. Some time ago, in another country, on the end of a telephone line, she had been amazed that Jaime had got his battered old Seat for free. After just a few days back in Andalucia it had become apparent why the car dealer had been so generous: where temperatures are regularly reaching 45 degrees centigrade, there is no market for black cars without air-conditioning. Jaime put on a Tom Jones cassette. He adored Tom Jones. He threw her glances as he sang to her and Seren smiled obligingly, while her soul clambered over the prickly pears in the surrounding shrub-land.

When they reached sea level, the land in the distance was swamped. A shining pool had flooded the road ahead. An aged truck rumbled towards the water, its dusty reflection spilling over the ground between them. The road was wide and the earth on either side was bare and well worn. They passed a sign, El Rocio 3Km. Soon, there was just the expanse of water between them and the truck. Shimmering particles began to rise up from the truck's reflection. They rose into the air from the edge inwards, peeling back the pool and consuming the water. The water disappeared rapidly and completely.

Dry grit, kicked up by the truck, took the moisture

from the roof of Seren's mouth and the car lurched sideways. The truck passed by in a shroud of dust.

Jaime delighted in her amazement.

'The water, it's a mirage. Have you never seen one before?'

El Rocio was like the mirage, in that it did and it didn't exist. Jaime told her it had been built around a church whose Virgin was said to have special powers. At the same time each year, the faithful from all over Spain made a pilgrimage by foot, horse or cart. For those few days, the place was five families to a house and pulsed with life. Today, the houses were desolate and the air was at rest.

They parked the car in front of the only café. It was a long, wooden pre-fab that had been extended many times. All its shutters were down. A dog sat outside being hounded by flies. Next to him was a rack of dusty postcards. The gabble of a tv, accompanied by the drone of a large, commercial fridge, floated out to them through an open door. Jaime asked her if she'd like anything to drink.

'Uh, no,' she replied, thirsty but put off by the agitated dog. She smiled at Jaime and suggested that they go and see the Virgin. He took her hand and they walked to the church.

El Rocio rose from the earth, vast and white against the azure sky. An old, brown leathery man with a satchel sat nestled in the church's marble skirts. Seren imagined that he was collecting contributions. As they passed him, he shouted at them to buy a lottery ticket.

Inside the church, she found that the Virgin was indeed

beautiful. Catholic imagery often made Seren tearful. It
wasn't that it brought anything to mind; in fact her mind
went blank but always the same feeling. At Semana Santa
earlier that year, she had stood alone and wept as countless
processions of the Passion slowly united to fill the narrow
streets of Santa Cruz: suffering borne on the backs of the
people.

Before they left the church, she lit a candle for her
grandmother, the only Catholic she knew. She had a
tentative feeling that people were only supposed to light
candles for the dead, but she went ahead and did it
anyway. Jaime took a few steps towards Seren, reached for
her hand and held it firmly. After a few silent moments,
they turned and walked back out into the daylight. When
they reached the car, he slipped his sunglasses on and
grinned at her. She felt that, maybe, the distance between
them could close.

They drove on to Matalascanas. In less than an hour,
the Atlantic rose into view. They staked a claim to a patch
of sand and spent the rest of the day on the beach, dozing,
eating and drinking. Before they left they swam. The water
was cool, smooth and heavy. It kneaded and rolled their
limbs then laid them out on the shore to be slowly baked
dry by the fading sun.

Jaime and Seren packed the day away into the boot of the
car and cruised through darkness and silence back to the
city. Seren began to consider the cause and effect of the
lack of words between them. Before journeying half way to
a conclusion, her focus escaped her, settling instead on the

moonlit silhouettes of the rough, black hills. She searched the horizon for El Toro, the huge, two-dimensional, metal sculpted bull. When she saw him, he seemed to turn his head towards her, scattering the stars. He snorted playfully; his free, hot breath evaporating in the moonlight, singing a psalm of solitude.

When Jaime took the slip road into Los Pajaritos, a LED sign proclaimed, in red needlepoint, that it was 29 degrees centigrade. Walking through the night streets back to Jaime's flat, Seren avoided looking down at the pavement. She concentrated on the warm breeze touching her skin. The dim light had sharpened her senses and the air felt far softer in the darkness, a smooth, liquid velvet. They passed few other people but laughter and chatter drifted to meet them through open windows and doors.

As they turned the corner into Calle Golondrina, there were still a few children running around outside the bar, playing a kind of hopscotch over the drain covers, while their parents chain-smoked, sweated over their tapas and jeered at the television. Seren and Jaime stopped for a drink. Seren was handed a beer in a dirty glass. Jaime stroked her cheek with an open hand. His palm was greasy and she took her time to lift her eyes from the glass. Above their heads hung a sinewy jamon. Droplets of fat, stained with nicotine, dripped, dragged down the cured flesh. She forced a few sips of beer, made an attempt at a joke and then they left.

When they got back to the flat, the division between them was palpable and now it seemed irrevocable. A few misunderstood words were exchanged across the sexless chasm now separating their bodies, then they each closed a bedroom door behind them.

Seren lay on a mattress on the floor. The window was wide open and the metal shutter down. The air hung above her, pitch and molten. She stared into space, her eyes playing tricks on her as they adjusted to the dark. Finally, Seren surrendered to instinct. Tomorrow she would shed her skin and go back home.

Cardiff

Seren walked out of the airport to be baptised by the rain, just as she had been oppressed by the un-ending, clear blue skies of Andalucia. Her senses were at home with seasons and her gaze appreciated the subtle greys of the Glamorgan clouds. She took a taxi back into the city, thinking about the resolute silence that had met her when she told Jaime that she was leaving him. He had dropped a timetable of buses to Malaga airport next to her morning coffee cup, kissed her on the head and left for work.

Seren knelt shivering in her porchway and fumbled around in her luggage for her front door key. Cold rain dripped onto her eyelids. She was bemused to see a plastic bag left tucked up against the wall. She reached over and opened it. Inside were two records. One she had loaned to a friend, at least a year before, and perhaps by way of an apology, there was another record.

'DJ Shadow. What Does Your Soul Look Like?'

Seren hadn't heard of the artist but she was warmed by the homecoming gesture and smiled as she unlocked the door. Without taking off her coat, she walked into the front room, switched on the electricity and put the record on the turntable. As it began to spin, she turned away, leaned over and shook the rain from her hair.

A man's voice began to speak faintly, from a distance, gradually coming closer.

'In a few moments you will have an experience, which will seem completely real. It will be the result of your subconscious fears transformed to your conscious awareness. You have five seconds to terminate this record. Five, four, three, two, one....'

A beat swung in. Seren stood up straight and threw back her hair. The spinning words approached her in weightless steps and her mind stopped rotating.

'There's a game out there, and the stakes are high,
and the guy who runs it figures the averages all day long
and all night long.
Once in a while he lets you steal away,
but if you stay in the game long enough,
you've got to lose,
and once you lose, there's no way back.
No way back at all.'

Seren lifted the needle from the record and slid it back into the cover. She went into the kitchen, opened the fridge door and looked inside. It was empty.

Twelve Beer Blues

Tristan Hughes

Dav called it a beer downer. It visited in the afternoon, anytime between twelve and two, depending on the night before. There was no getting away from it. Once it arrived it clung to you as steadfastly as the tobaccoed fuzz on your teeth. A hangover was just a headache, a troubled coil of guts, but the beer downer was a malaise, a metaphysical predicament. There was no aspirin or alka-seltzer in the world that would make it go away. Dylan had learnt to spot the auguries of its coming: you stopped laughing – what seemed funny in the leftover drunkenness of morning suddenly wasn't – you wanted to be alone, you wanted to phone everyone you'd met the night before and say sorry, you wanted to slip away forever into the shadows.

It was in the shadows that the beer downer lived. It liked you to be alone with it. Once there was only you and it, then it could begin:

'What were you like last night?'

'I wus fine.'

'You were a wanker.'

'Didn't you talk to her last night?'

'Yeh. We got on a-right. I think she quite likes me.'

'She thinks you're a nob.'

'Did you cop off with anyone last night?'

'No.'

'Then what exactly do you call what you were doing with Pamela?'

The downer always got the better of these conversations; there was no point in arguing with it. It was a surly know-it-all, a bleak and bullying sophist. It lorded it over you, a connoisseur of abjection and anxiety, decanting them like vinegary wines and forcing you to drink from the bitter, bile-tinctured cup.

Eleven o'clock said Dylan's watch, Saturday said the calendar in the corner, one hour to go he said to himself.

*

It would have helped if he'd known where exactly he was. The room was unfamiliar. He was lying on a purple settee, a dark, wet patch beside his mouth where the drool had flowed through the night. There were empty cans on the coffee table in front of him, rising up from the mug-ringed surface like an avenue of miniature skyscrapers; STELLA called out the crimson-edged insignia on their sides, throbbing through the dull morning light like neon.

STELLA. In the streets below there were heaps of ash and the crumpled brown of fag butts. This tiny city was still asleep. Outside the window another one was awake.

Pulling open the curtains made hardly any difference to the light. The gloom of January flowed in, the gloom of the morning after flowed out. They were almost the same. A car pulled away below him; the noise of its engine ricocheted off the sloping line of slate roofs opposite. It was such a small place. One landmark would be enough.

From the corner of the room came the sound of coughing. Dylan looked over and saw the scrunched shape of a body wrapped in a white sheet, twitching like a larva in a cocoon, waiting to be reborn. The coughing intensified, the sheet fell away, Dav opened a pair of pink, vein-tendrilled eyes and then started blinking, bemusedly, at the world around him. It took him a while to recognise Dylan, and a while longer to speak:

'Where the fokk are we?'

'Dunno.'

'We're in Bangor, yeh?'

'Course we fokking are. I jus dunno where, like.'

'I've been freezing mu tits off all night, s'a miracle I'm still alive, mate.'

'More's the pity.'

Just the one would be enough. Beyond the uppermost tier of slates loomed a hill, covered in a ragged blanket of dead bracken, its faded orange as dull as the sky. To the right, cut in half by the window frame, was the grey smudge of the mountains.

'Caernarfon road, somewhere, I reckon.'

'I reckon yer right, mate,' said Dav, rising unsteadily onto his feet and stretching out his arms. The bright colours of his shirt unfurled in the failing light.

The door opened, and in walked Iestyn Bell-End, beaming.

'You were quite a pair last night,' he said, laughing. He loved it when you made a cock of yourself; it drew all the attention away from him, who usually did.

'A-right Iest,' Dav croaked, unsettling thirty fags' worth of sediment in his throat. 'Where the ell are we?'

'This is my flat.'

'Since when?'

'Since when? Since I moved ere two months ago, you idiut; since you bloody well helped me move in, you daft bugger.'

'O aye. I'd fergotten that.'

'Idiut.'

Eleven fifteen, said the clock. Somewhere in the back of Dylan's head, approximately below his ears, a cloud seemed to be forming. It had started off as the merest speck, a tiny jangling mote, but had now expanded into a swirling, nebulous mass. Within it, various images were beginning to take shape. They fizzed like comets through the revolving murk, none of them definite yet, none of them clear, but each of them gathering density and clarity with alarming speed. One of them was becoming, all too distinctly, the back yard of Chukkies. Soon he could make out the big plastic skips, heaped full of beaks and slithery, steaming innards; the clotted pools of blood, matted over with feathers, and the crooked, beckoning claws. A dead

eye looked out at him from beneath a crown of drooping
red. And then, suddenly, there was Pamela's face: pale,
powdered and cratered like the surface of a moon, the thin,
pink slits of her lips parted in inebriated expectation. Then
a glass breaking. A flurry of fists and the strained tendons
on Dav's neck as he screamed obscenities. And then her,
smiling. If only he could make that one stay still, if only he
could stop the others.

But he couldn't. The only option was to out-run them,
to match their momentum with his own.

'Come on, Dav, let's get a move on.'

'Where?'

'Home, yu nob.'

*

Outside on the street, Iestyn, who'd decided to come with
them to the bus-stop, started to act out the night before.
He played all the parts, jerking and jumping and gesturing
his way down the pavement like a walking, one-man
pantomime. Dav discovered a lump on his forehead, just
beneath the soft bristle of his hair, and Iestyn leapt towards
him, brandishing a theatrical fist.

'Got yu right there, mate. An he wus a massive bastard
too, wusn't he Dyl?'

'Yeh.'

'Don't remember,' said Dav, feeling his head.

Iestyn replayed the punch again and thought it was
hilarious. Two old women on the opposite pavement eyed
them all suspiciously.

They'd come to the railway bridge and as they passed under it, Dylan felt the shadows wrap themselves around him. On the other side, the light was too weak to dissolve them. A sign on the front of a shop to their right proclaimed Penryn Monumental Works. Above it rose a huge, and suitably monumental, gravestone; standing like an Easter Island god on the roof, it looked back towards the mountains from which it had once been chiselled, and forward towards where the main street snaked down into the city centre and then on into the sea. Dylan got the strange feeling it was watching him and tried to hide himself behind the others. It was no use: however he positioned himself he couldn't shake its stone eyes. Neither could he shake the desire to hide. As they made their way further down the street he glanced frantically down alleyways and side-roads, into the windows of empty restaurants and abandoned shops, through the expectant, just opened doors of pubs, anywhere that might conceal him.

The night before it had been so different. In the back seat of a mate's car they'd edged their way around the island's shore towards the bridge, drinking cans of lager and staring across the straits towards the city. There'd been music playing, and each note had seemed to quicken their heartbeats, and each word of the songs had seemed somehow full of possibility and promise, like a girl whispering in your ear. And as they'd hurtled over the bridge, closer to the welcoming glow of the street lamps, it had felt as though they were leaving everything behind them in the darkness, that there was nothing but the hours that glimmered and sparkled in front.

Pamela saw them first. She was standing on the pavement beside a rack of discounted shoes, putting nylon slippers into the Must Go bucket at its side. Iestyn and Dav casually slowed down, and then gave Dylan a none too subtle shove to make sure he was in front. She looked at him and started to smile, but the impulse became mixed with second and third thoughts and the smile came out an awkward, twisted grimace. She dropped a handful of slippers onto the pavement. Dylan wished he wasn't here, then he panicked and wondered if he should smile, then he decided he should but wasn't sure if that was enough and so decided to say hello as well.

'A-rright,' he mumbled, but by then they were a good ten yards past her.

Dave pushed an elbow into his ribs.

'She's minging fer Wales, mate.'

'Wales! She's minging for the fucking universe!' shouted Iestyn, loud enough for most of it to hear him.

Dylan wished they'd leave her alone. She was nice, really, and talking about her like this made him feel secretly bad. He wished he'd let her alone – then she wouldn't have been part of this conversation and he wouldn't feel guilty. But those first hours had been a golden blur and everything he'd poured into his belly had worked like the gift of Midas. In the Castell the lights had been loud and kind, and every song had been the one he most wanted to hear and every smile was aimed at him, and Pamela hadn't looked so bad – even Iestyn had seemed funny. In the blur there were no befores and afters, no hours or minutes or days, only moments and seconds; you were in them, and then you were out of them, and why and how you got there didn't matter. In one of them his lips were pressed against Pamela's, in another her tongue was pushing back his own. Then she was gone and the pub had vanished. Dav and Iestyn and him had been walking down the street, laughing, and had carried on walking, right through the doors of Bliss.

*

From the top of the tower the hands of the clock said quarter to twelve. It was right there, in the middle of town, and there was no getting away from it. It could see everything; you couldn't help but see it.

'Let's go down past the chippy,' said Dylan.

'Fuck that, it's longer that way,' said Iestyn.

'Come on, I'm starving,' said Dylan. He wasn't. But down there you couldn't see it.

Across the road from the chippy was Bliss. Dylan bit into a chip, or rather the chip dissolved onto his teeth, coating them in a salty, oily mush. Trying to keep his attention directed firmly away from what was sliding into his belly, Dylan surveyed the building opposite. There was no denying it: in the failed light of day, Bliss looked like a shithole. The walls had become blocks of crumbling grey concrete; the doors had closed, revealing a coating of flaking black paint; on the pavement outside, where the night before there'd been a line of people talking and shouting and laughing, there was now a queue of silent skips, their mouths clogged full of empty bottles. An old poster on the front proclaimed Hawaiian Night in weak yellow letters; beneath them was a faded patch of tropical sky and a row of drooping palms. Under the palms a girl danced a half-hearted hula, her eyes apparently fixed in disgust on a streak of vomit that was smeared against the fronds of her grass skirt.

'She's looking at yu,' Iestyn had said.

'Get away,' he'd said.

'I'm not joking or nuthing, yeh; she's staring at yu!'

'Stop moidering, will yu.'

But he'd desperately hoped he wasn't. He'd spotted her the moment they'd got to the bar, leaning against a steel railing at the edge of the dance floor, holding a bottle of something unnaturally blue. Behind her the lights had pulsed across peoples' bodies, holding them for a second – with their arms stretched up into the air and their heads tilted at odd angles – and then letting them go again, back into the briefest blinks of darkness. In between these little eclipses he'd made out her features: the pale crescent of her forehead; the gentle rise of her cheekbones and the shadowed skin beneath; the slightly convex curve of her bottom lip. For a while he'd felt as though here at the bar, beyond the reach of the lights, he was somehow invisible; and then he'd searched out her eyes and found they were pointed back at him. Bollocks, he'd thought; I'm leering like some kind of perv. For a second he'd wished the darknesses would last longer.

'Well, if yer not going tu do nothing then I'm goin tu giv it a go,' Iestyn slurred.

'Ah come on, Iest, leave it out, will yu.'

But it was too late; Iestyn was already lurching over towards her.

'Yer a fokking liability you are, Iest,' Dylan blurted out, before staggering after him. They'd left Dav at the bar, haggling pointlessly over three pints of Stella.

In the ten seconds or so it took Dylan to catch up with him, Iestyn had already made a good start of humiliating himself. He'd launched into a kind of high-speed jabbering, unleashing a torrent of pissed syllables that flowed into each other to become one continuous stream of mangled and incoherent sound, punctuated only by the frantic, beseeching movement of his hands. It was a real Bell-End performance. Vintage. The look on her face was half confusion, half fear. By the time Dylan arrived, he could tell she was happy to see him. Iestyn had sloped off onto the dance floor, to hide himself in other sounds.

'Sorry about him,' Dylan said.

'Christ, what's he on,' she said.

'He's always like that, when he's pissed, yeh. An when he's sober too, a bit like.'

And she'd smiled then.

Only seconds and moments, but these ones had felt different. He hadn't wanted them to pass. There was nothing in them that would make him feel guilty, that could make him feel ashamed. And then she'd asked him what he did, and the beaks and blood and claws had come cavorting into his head, ready to spoil everything. But by now he was too drunk to lie.

'I work at Chukkies.'

'Oh, right. So what you do there, then?'

'I kill chickens.'

Only moments and seconds, and he'd thought that maybe these ones were over, that this was the end of them and he'd have to leave them go and move on into others. He was watching her face for a sign, but there didn't seem to be one. She just said: 'That must be a bit grim.'

'Yeh, it's awful.'

And then they had moved on into others, in a way he hadn't been expecting. Afterwards, for the first time that night, all he'd been able to think of was what had been before.

To begin with he hadn't even noticed Dav standing behind him. Then he'd heard him, talking to some big lad he played football with.

'...so yer saying mu lef' foot's shite.'

'Nah, I'm jus saying yu'd be better on the right, like.'

'So yer saying I'm a wanker.'

'Fokk off, will yu, I'm not saying that...'

'So yer tellin' us to fokk off are yu...'

'No... I'm jus saying yu'd...'

'Twat!'

Dylan turned around just in time to see Dav's forehead jerk forward into the lad's chest. About a minute later, Dav was lying on the floor surrounded by broken glass. About two minutes later they were out on the street.

*

The bus arrived spot on at twelve o'clock. They waved Iestyn goodbye with a couple of 'v's out the back window as it pulled away. Dav fell instantly into a pale silence and stared down at his shoes; they were covered in the sticky remains of various spilt alcopops. They moved up the road, past the train station and towards the upper part of town, passing students and Saturday shoppers and old women carrying plastic baskets. Behind them the bulging line of mountains receded like a constellation of grey, setting suns. And then all the people and houses had gone and there were only the straits and the dull green shore of the island. They were getting home.

After crossing the bridge the bus stopped everywhere. It seemed like every time they went past more than two houses it would grind to a halt, wait while nobody got on, wait until nobody got off, and then rumble on for another mile or two. The night before it had been like they'd just flowed into town, but this bus ride back was like one long stalling and stuttering bunny-hop. And every time they stopped, Dylan knew he was getting closer. It looked like he'd caught up with Dav already, who was now staring down at his shoes so miserably that it appeared as though he were planning to wash them with his tears. Sometimes he took on odd shapes and forms. Usually it was his mother or father. But once it had been his dinner lady from primary school – who'd forced him to eat tinned tomatoes as a child, even though they made him puke – and another time it had been his old reg teacher, Mrs Jones, who had faintly purple hair and taught RE and had, on more than one occasion, insinuated that he'd end up in hell. Lately, though, he'd begun to appear in the guise of giant cockerel, often with an eye missing. He wished the driver would just keep moving.

Eventually Dylan could stand it no longer. They'd come to a pair of houses on the shore, about two miles from the village, and when the bus stopped this time, he got up to get off.

'See yu, mate,' he said.

'See yu,' said Dav, barely even lifting his head.

As the bus pulled away, Dylan walked quickly down towards the sea. He sat on a rock and watched it. It looked like a huge pool of undulating oil. The sound of it washing against the stones beneath his feet was like the smooth rustle of feathers. He was waiting for him now, there was no point hiding anymore. But for a second he began to think of her instead, of how she hadn't gone away, and how afterwards nothing had felt like it was wrong.

'What were you like last night,' he said.

'I wus fine. I wus a-right. I wus happy.'

And, for a moment, he was.

Freshers' Week

Niall Griffiths

There is a hill to the south of Aberystwyth called Pen Dinas. Permanently atop it is a tall thin pillar, a monument to the Napoleonic War built by a one-armed veteran of that conflict and today clustered around it is a crowd of people say thirty in number and all with one exception of first-year student age, say early twenties. The exception is a man in his mid-thirties standing central to the larger group and clapping his hands for attention amongst the chatter. Seagulls call all forlorn behind the exuberant voices and waves can be heard faintly crashing, somewhere below on the shore.

– Okay everyone... okay... listen up now...

The chatter slowly dies. The older man continues:
– I'd like to welcome you all to Aberystwyth, university and town, and congratulate you on your decision to study by

the sea. As you probably know, as part of your freshers' week activities, today is a tour of the town conducted by my good self, congenial host and student also, albeit mature one, and –

– And boring bastard! A heckler calls out, to much laughter and further heckling. It is good-natured and taken in that vein by the tourguide and is delivered in that affected faux-Cockney manner evidently common to all students now, regardless of their class or geographical origins. They all talk the same. They have far less accentual diversity than the gulls thinly crying overhead, borne by the wind multi-tongued. The guide continues: – And very boring bastard, yes. Incredibly dull. Standing here on this hill called Pen Dinas, anyone know what that means in English?

– Den's Penis!

More laughter.

– Lucky fackin Den, eh!

– Lucky Den's fackin missis!

– It means 'head of the city'. Because, as you can see, the town ends all that way below you against the foot of this very hill. It's not a natural hill, or not all of it anyway; it was an Iron Age fortress, built by people who had some kind of trade agreement with Ireland, directly opposite us over the sea there. They –

More heckling: – What's the big monument for?

– It's a model of my dick. Liiiifesize!

Laughter.

– It was built by a veteran of the Napoleonic War. He only had one arm and he built all that by himself, just him and a donkey. Incredible, eh?

– Stupid more like.

– Yeah. Didn't he have anything better to do, this geezah?

– Why did he bother?

– Cos he was a tosser.

– Nah, the guide says, he just wanted a monument, a commemoration, like. Wanted people to know what he'd been through, the horrors he'd seen, and to honour all the dead.

– Horrors! Plenty of them in France, man.

General laughter and agreement. The guide continues: – Down there you can see the castle. Not much of it left now, but you can just make out –

– My puke from last night.

– Yeah! A ton of empty bottles!

– Which weren't empty when we started, man, eh?

– Quality, my bravvah, quality!

– It changed hands between the Welsh and the English on several occasions. After the last time, which I think was during the Glyndŵr wars of rebellion, the townsfolk took a lot of the stone and built their own houses with it, which is why, if you look at the streets leading up from the harbour, you can see –

– Yawn, yawn! Get on wiv it, geezah!

– Show us the pubs!

– Yeah, man! Where are the pubs!

– The boozahs, my bravvah!

– And if you look at the Old College there, see, beyond the castle by the big church? See the murals on the gable end?

– Oh very exciting...

A new voice sounds: a female voice. It is genuinely inquisitive: – Can I ask you a question?

– What?

– Can I ask you a question?

– Fire away.

– What's the point of this?

– The point? Well, the point is just to introduce you to the town, like. Welcome you to Aberystwyth kind of thing, point out the sights, the places of interest.

– The pubs! Point out the pubs!

– It's full of history. The human history of this place is fascinating. It's a town on the edge of the world.

The female voice again: – No, what I mean is, what's the point of this for you? Why are you doing this? Is it part of your, erm, duties as a guide or do you just enjoy it?

– Well it's not officially part of me duties like but...

– You're not from round here, are you?

– No, I was born in Liverpool. But I've lived here for years.

– Why did you move here?

– The pub! We wanna go the pub!

– Well, not to put too fine a point on it... I was a waster. There was a time in me life when I used a hell of a lot of drugs. A hell of a lot.

– Not as much as me!

– Mate, no one smokes as much as you.

Laughter. A great deal of laughter.

The female voice continues: – Yeh, so? Why Aberystwyth?

– Don't really know. I was just, y'know, escaping, trying to get away from the places that were bad for me.

Bad influences, like. Once you get to know the town you'll hear a lot of similar stories from people like me, who just came here to get away from the mess they'd made of their lives. Come from all over the country, they do. You'll hear a lot of different accents in this small town.

    – So there's a lot of drugs around then?

    – Hope so!

    – Not for long, with us around!

    – Too right, geezah!

    – And I mean... well, all these people, they come here by the sea to get away from their problems but they end up bringing their problems with them. So you've got this big and diverse collection of screwed-up people in a little town like this and... well let's just say that some people don't survive.

There is mocking laughter. Much of it. Some of these voices here, these young voices, can be heard to actually scoff. One, even, harrumphs, and says: – I'm from London, my bravvah. Naffin you can tell me abaht this stuff that I don't already know.

    – I lived in Putney in my teens, the guide responds. – Which part of London are you from?

    – Guildford, man, yeah!

    – Some stories we could tell you, for sure.

    – And some I could tell you, n all. Anyway, if –

    – Go on, then!

    – What?

    – Tell us a story.

    – I already am. I'm telling you some of the history of what in my opinion is one of the most intriguing towns in the British Isles. I've travelled all over this country and I tell you, I've –

More heckling, much mocking laughter. It is beginning to acquire an edge. Unsharp as yet, unhoned it is, but an edge nevertheless.

– He ain't got none!

– Yeah. Smoked a few spliffs in your time, av ya?

– Dropped an E one time at Glasto?

Jeering. This goes on for some moments as the older man waits indulgently, patiently. As it dies he resumes speaking, his voice still level, calm: – So you've all quite finished, now? Right. I'll continue. On the far side of the town, directly opposite us, see that other big hill? That's called Constitution Hill. The funicular that leads to the summit is the longest one in Europe and –

– Nah, man! We want a story!

– Yeah! Story!

They begin to chant: – Story! Story! Story! Story!

– Yeah! We want the personal touch, geezah!

– Story! Story! Story!

The chanting goes on for some time until the guide's voice snaps and becomes abruptly hard: – Alright. Youse all want a story? I'll give yiz a fuckin story. The heckling abruptly stops. The only voices now are the wind and gulls and crashing waves. – Turn around. Go on, all of youse, turn around.

There is a shuffling as many feet turn.

– Now. See that long road leading up out of the town, up the hill past the university? See it?

Some mumbled agreement, the students evidently

cowed by the hardness in the man's voice now. – Now see the house about halfway up, the one painted bright yellow?

Some mumbled agreement again.

– Well when I first arrived here that house wasn't yellow. It was the colour of grime and d'yis know why? Cos it was a squat. It was lying empty and a bunch of wasters from all over the place decided to squat it. And there was a couple who lived in there who came from Swansea, let's call them Betty and Wayne, and Betty and Wayne were very much in love.

A pause; gulls and wind and waves. – And I mean really in love; they absolutely doted on each other. Never have I, before or since, seen a couple who loved each other as much as Wayne and Betty did. They did everything together and managed to turn it all into an exciting adventure: signing on, boiling the kettle, watching telly, going to the shop, everything to them was full of excitement and wonder cos they were so much in love. Oh yeh, they were wasters, drop-outs like, even junkies – I mean Betty had had an intravenous habit for four or five years when I first met her – but that doesn't mean they couldn't feel genuine love, does it? Well, not unless you're a *Daily Mail* reader, anyway. I mean these people were meant for each other; they were both caring, kind, gentle towards children and animals and those worse off than themselves and generous? God, yes, to a fault; they'd share their last meal with you. And they did, once or twice. Oh yeh; beans and potatoes, that's all they had, but they made sure I had something hot in me belly after I'd been sleeping rough all night under the pier.

Pause.

– Then one day Betty was gone. No warning or anything, she was just gone. I called round at the squat and there's Wayne on his own in tears in the room he shared with Betty and it was disturbing seeing Wayne without his arm around Betty cos they seemed like the same organism, Siamese twins or something, cos you never saw them without their arms round each other. So it upset me, like, to see Wayne on his own. I asked him where Betty was and he said he didn't want to talk about it so fair enough, I thought, she's left him; only goes to show that you can't rely on anything in this world, this life. Even something seemingly as solid as their relationship can break down and fall apart. You should never rely on anything. There are no constants. Except hope, of course, and I kept calling round there, hoping that Betty had come back but no, nothing doing, just Wayne on his own growing increasingly withdrawn day by day, not eating, wasting away, not washing or cleaning his room and the smell got so bad that I eventually stopped calling round there, as did everybody else; I mean Wayne never left his room and the stink in there had gotten unbearable. And the flies, God, his room was beginning to fill with flies. No one could stand it anymore; Wayne's misery and the stench and the flies. And one day, according to the other squatters like, Wayne locked his door and refused to open it. Wouldn't even speak through it, wouldn't come out for food, nothing. Just locked himself away from the world. Until the smell began to permeate the whole house and the other squatters couldn't stand it anymore so they kicked the door down and... no

Wayne. The room was empty. Or that's what they thought until they looked under the bed.

Pause.

Betty had been dead for weeks. She'd OD'd. And Wayne had hidden her under the bed because – and he'd left a suicide note explaining all this – he couldn't bear the thought of being away from her. Couldn't handle the thought of her being buried or burned. So he kept her under the bed and at night-time he'd take her out and tuck her under the covers and read stories to her, her favourite science-fiction stories like, and then one day when he'd had enough and I suppose she'd become too, erm, you know... well, he decided to follow her. Decided to kill himself. But he had no drugs cos he hadn't been out the house for weeks and no one had visited him neither – which is the part that's always puzzled me cos it means he must've cold turkeyed and kicked the drugs and been of a clear head when he did what he did – and he had no knife to slit his wrists, no rope to hang himself so he... he ate the mattress. Or part of it, anyway; tore it open with his teeth and ate the stuffing till he couldn't breathe anymore and it expanded in his stomach and he choked and died. So he could be with Betty. But the final touch, like, the last detail, is that Wayne was dressed in a smart black suit and Betty, what was left of her like, was in a wedding dress. Veil and everything. None of us even knew they were married. We thought they were like us, just wasters.

Long pause. Only the wind and the waves.

– So there's yer story. And now look at me; I'm a mature student studying theatre choreography and lighting.

I'm a valuable and sensible citizen and a decent human being who's repented of his ways and all that kind of happy stuff and things like that don't happen to me anymore. I'm just a... just a...

He trails off, doesn't finish the sentence. A gull sounds, quite loudly, and in the mourning of its call is all thwarted reaching, all disappointment on the earth.

– Okay, so follow me. There's some fascinating geology on the south beach it would be edifying for you all to see.

He walks away. After a few moments the others follow silently but just a few moments later as the unique grit-stone formations on the foreshore are being pointed out, the heckling voices begin to rise again. This is boring, they say. We wannah go the pub. All in that fictitious accent which comes from no real place and which never seems to change.

chupa mi pena, baby

lloyd robson

strange, how the body remembers the act. how articulate
the hands of an ex-smoker remain when handed baccy &
rizla & lump of black. how invasive memories of childhood
drive the facial muscles back to an expression long lost
or make the arsehole contract. moscow diesel, henna,
cack. bits of rope. sea spoil, salted & damp. or dried to
crust & cracks. the spread of young legs. the speed of
the mind. not fast enough to escape the past. the spark of
a flint. goes out. smoke in. in. held. an adult not sharp
enough to get away. out. the adult brain too tired & too
sick of the sight. look in the mirror & see some fat-arse drag
act who's bored of it all but still lites up the nite with a
superstar smile by queen's command. the eyes. the lines
the cake can't hide. the painted mouth beams back at her,
reminds her of an ex-boyfriend's parting riposte: 'ladylike?

you got a gob like a bulldog's twat.' & that was the end of
that.

'ladies & gentlemen, the star of the nite...'

lady moneydown stands up. downs her pint. lowers
the ride of her dress around hips, her waist pulled tight.
fingers her straps. leaves the girls in the changing room &
strides to the wings. hands her spliff to the the dj & picks
up a mic. 'good evening you lovely, lovely people! oh you
all look gorgeous, i do hope some of you are single....'

the lites go down, the gig is up. the club's jam-packed
with lovers, lechers & limberers up. shit-thick at the bar,
it's catcalls & mine's a pint. straight & gay mix, shouting
orders to staff. bulk supplies of local cocktails 'our shirl's
spit' & 'going down in the castle grounds'. extra-size office
workers bulge fancy dress uniforms & drag from their
handbags disposable cameras to capture hen party laffs.
hands full of cocktails & piss beer; urine-gold lager & fizzy
bitter. hands full of hans, the austrian nursing student
fool enough to be entrapped by their charms, sovereigned
fingers & gold-plate earrings. an evening out for the girls,
away from the usual haunts of the combined clubs skittles
league, runners-up for the last two years but currently
leaving behind the chasing pack. they'll still spend the nite
in the city's gutters & alleys. vomiting, fucking, or hailing
a cab. the fotos will capture their red eyes perfectly. the
bride-to-be in her white veil & red bull stains, dragging a
blow-up by his limp plastic dick. the wedding will go
perfectly, the reception & disco drunkenly, the wedding
nite a flop.

in this self-proclaimed hall of babylon, the preened &
perverse, the clamour for glamour & the attempts to get
served, bunch at the taps. spending cashplus & flicking
ash, reactions in the eyes of anxious ex-smokers & the
noses of ganj connoisseurs. alongside the nurses taking
a break from the philly, the frozen rose sellers making a
living, the prozzies on their way back to trade street & its
ins & outs. each stumbling over her own heels in the rush
to get a drink. each with personalised scram marks down
her back. squashed between this & the raised counter flap.

lady, as she calls herself, stands on stage & grins.
tasselled like they never seen she steals a line from
baudelaire; steals a line from a pretentious french poetry-
loving one-nite, one very short nite, stand. all limp dick &
beer. 'clad in her undulating pearly dress'. ah yes. she
grins. a change from the necklace she normally gives, the
pearls of wisdom she offers her guests as she straddles
them under her sheets. she likes em fit, but she gets em fat.
men with breasts many women would envy. there's a lot to
be said for an eager fat lovely, fat spanky. they work hard
to get what they get. fucking chubby chaser now, who'd
believe it. back to the set: 'is there a darren in tonite? i've
got a message from your fiancée darren – she'd speak for
herself but she's got her mouth full right now....'

the boys laff, the girls cheer.

'seriously though love, where you from? jesusfuck-
agypsy he's from swansea. well congratufuckinlations
darren my darling, her waters broke so you'd better run. go
on! run, run like the wind. & you boys who fancy him, you
better mince, mince like the breeze. he won't get far with

his jeans round his ankles. no, your mother-in-law phoned darren, she knew you'd be here. turning into a right regular aren't you, only you don't usually bring your friends along. not this crowd anyroad. she sounds a right miserable bitch, your mother-in-law. still, bitter is the clitoris which doesn't get its fix....'

in the swallow club she's doing all right. not great, but survives. plenty of flirting, two shows a nite. last year she had the weekend, the prime party slots, but lady moneydown has been pushed aside. not surprising really, considering the club now plays host to *meat magritte*: a fifteen-strong troop; *full monty* meets the surrealist movement kinda show. no, more than a show: an audience participatory exotic strip event, shipped over from the continent, aimed at the new, informed wealthy & the college-taught cheap. an opportunity to hang strapping great men from the ceiling wearing nothing more than bowler hats & dirty macs & sparkly posing pouches. their umbrellas up, they are lowered into the audience to the strains of *it's raining men*. hallelujah! the hen parties & gay gangs go crazy. the men get groped to shreds. yes, groped to shreds. up close they're all grab marks & bruising.

'this one's for all you piercing fans who are suffering from allergy rash. yes, it's diana ross' *chain reaction*. come on then, up & dance....' she points stubby toes in stilettos & blasts her lungs.

clambering on stage, a grabber ladders her tights. 'don't you go touching me, my pretty' she sez, 'less you got money in your hand. & it's no good jiggling the coins in your pocket like that – i don't come cheap; i come writhing

& screaming like a banshee with a jack hammer up her
arse. but then you know that already dear – bet you haven't
told your mates that....'

the crowd love it. his mates lap it up. she turns away
& wiggles her arse. 'remember that don't you, eh? he
couldn't get enough. but it was over very quickly wasn't it
love. never mind. then he went back to the bar & before i
knew it he had a mouthful of john smith's – you daren't
turn your back on the man...'

his mates shout back. she doesn't hear. he takes the
laff.

'tonite's music is for the girls who have been there,
caught that, but now it's cleared up. yes, we're gonna sing
for you tina turner's *warts love got to do with it*, followed
by the theme tune to *from thrusha with love*, & finishing off
with elvis' *hunka hunka burning love*. go on then girls, give
it a good scratch...'

she hates these cunts. especially those who dance.
those who view this as *la nuit exotique*. slappers & tramps,
not an ounce of class. bags, dags, hags, lags, blags, slags,
drags & glads. fucking hates her own material, the show,
the gags. makes an entrance, crude jokes, bad attempts at
impersonation, milks a quick promise of more to come &
exit stage right. a costume change then back for the
cabaret. get em joining in. up on stage if they're not too
drunk. when the poppers hit the air watch the virgins &
curious drop *en masse*. playing to a bunch of fat farts &
dozy kids born to a generation who think the birmingham
six are a boy band.

the spasm madams & tv tarts. the sauce pots & poxy

doxies, the honey cunnies, the radyr riders & splott slots. the eye magnets, the heart snatchers & money grabbers, the well-breasted chickies, the little-tittied ladies, the pretty girls with fat arses. the gangs of lads. the smoother movers off to get hammered, out tomming the town. those who wear aftershave only after a match, getting away from another nite sat tissues in hand watching *suck my dog* or *madam cack*. the students, the doleheads, the glam, the sham, the seedy, the sexy, the spent, the done. the piss ants, spank rags, *schwätzers*, daft arabs, dozy born bastards, the clapt out. those who still live with their mams. the mother gifts, the second-wind nans. the hairy marys, the screaming wendys, the spunk puppets & lemon lesbians, the diesel dykes. the come up & see me some time. the under-dressed & over-crammed. the withdrawn amongst their gang. the warm & certain. the bubbling. the hot. the shovel-deep confidence of the determined & damned. the experienced or virginal. those looking for something untried. those who want a little bit. those who want it all. those who cannot look themselves in the eye. those who want to control. the sex terrorists. their hostages. those who define themselves by their ability to satisfy. some body else. those who have lost their self to the desires of the powerful. the lust of others. the enquiry, the secrecy, the don't tell anyone else. those who spend their lives in search of what can only ever be lost. those who are defined by what has happened in the past. those who are trapped. those who use sex to escape from themselves. those who gamble on lust reaching love. those who like to tie you up. those who like to be undone. those who invite the destruction. those who like to instruct. those who like to be in front. those who like to watch. those who during the nite will demand the spotlite as they get undressed: on stage, on the table, on the grass; laid on a cathays grave, the backseat, the new ikea work surface, even, in extreme cases, the marital bed. those who just love it love it love it & cannot get enough. those who just think it's all a big laff. & those who don't.

at the back of the club, a middle-aged woman launches herself onto a young man's lap (the last: the one to take years off her life) & grabs a handful of bollocks. he drops his glass. his girlfriend too polite to ask what the fuck she thinks she's doing with her private sweetmeats in her sweaty, ageing hand. drunk as she is, the woman will remember, regret, self chide. then remember how earlier, oh shit, her tongue in a young queen's mouth. how he struggled to escape. how his boyfriend complained. how she'll go home alone. how it's been so long since she woke with the warmth of a man, a cock pressed against her in the morning. a face between her legs, a tongue on her clitoris, someone to hear her glory moan. the make-up on her pillow. the day they eloped, years ago. the storming. the fights to the end. the day she came home to the note he wrote. how she tore it up but kept the pieces. how she cried. how she swore. how she dragged herself up & out of the door. how she humiliates herself, butchers herself in the search for some warmth. a kiss. hot on her neck. or a great big slobbery snog. an arm around her when she snores, someone to push her out of bed, into the shower, someone to watch her wash, someone to notice she's shaved her legs, someone to lite her cigarette, someone to dance naked in her kitchenette, someone to stop her getting old. or feeling it. so much of it. to stop her being alone.

back on stage: 'i've just got divorced. it was only a short marriage. it came to a head on our wedding nite when he told me he was already married. my friend said: "well that's big of him – admitting & that." i said: "big of him! it's bigamy!" the bastard....'

the glass-collector does her round. twenty-six she reckons, stacked & sticky. six fingers jammed into the necks of foreign beers. clears the tables, sick of the same fucking gags. gets really pissed off with slices of lime. a dolehead by day, she dreams of her own, imminent, meteoric rise. from beer cellar to interstellar, a superstar before their eyes. she totters through the yabbering throng with her tower of breakables; through the hen parties, the twenty-year-old girls with their making-up-time mams; barges through the office workers who popped in for the one & haven't left since, the valley boys here to take the piss but, secretly, to see for themselves the tight-topped queens, the bicurious, the in-between.

she walks past aristo in his booth, talking business with a slaughterhouse worker wearing neatly pressed jeans & a markzies shirt, blood in the reek of him & under his nails. they discuss developments in the dodgy meat racket. aristo's turned his hand & his catering contacts to selling condemned meat to the whole of cardiff. he's making a killing, he's carved up the market.

'so i got rid of that shit & i've replaced him with a younger model. yes i've got a new boyfriend & he's picking

me up later, so when george michael arrives do give him
room girls. no, seriously, i'm meeting my boyfriend later
– did i say *meat* him? well yes, that too. but my boyfriend
is gorgeous. & he thinks i'm gorgeous too. he first fell for
my long smooth legs. he got down on his knees & stroked
them gently up & down my calves, the back of my knees, my
thighs, slipping his hands up my dress. so i asked: "where's
your preference lie, with the left or the right?" & he
replied: "hmm, somewhere in-between." saucy bugger. he's
a wonderful man is my boyfriend. dirty, but wonderful.
knows his place though. down there with his mouth full. i
said to him: "what do you want for christmas?" he said: "a
word in edgeways." cheeky fucker, honest to god. they
soon forget the romance, don't they girls? his motto is "if
you like it, stroke it." speaking of legs though: children in
callipers, you don't see many of them any more....'

behind the bar, the maid's wig is slipping. underneath
she's eggshell blonde. when she bends for a bottle her
top rides up & her hipsters down, revealing a tattoo:
'revolution' etched above her fat arse. oil tankers turn
faster than she can. south american dictatorships are born
& dissolved before she gets to the fridge. by the time she's
got your lager open, the moon has slipped out of orbit &
the bottle top popped between her tits. she looks at you
coquettishly as she dives in & fishes. retrieves it & slides it
towards your hand. you lose your footing on the beer-
sloshed floor. the earth & the dancers shift on their poles,
tidal swellings crash full force. she hands over your drink,
now warm. menstrual women are no longer in sync, day &
nite are equally lit, amoebae are tap-dancing by the time

she's rung it in the till, spirogyra are up & walking, doing the conga, you hand over a fiver just before the volcanoes of wales are reborn, the mountains torn & we're all washed away by the severn bore. don't bother waiting for your change. no point. who's gonna say shit when her son is the six-four muscle working the door? & he's got mates.

having hovered & dodged for a quarter hour an executive officer from the llanishen tax office sidles up to the bar: 'the inclusion of unnecessarily collated statistical data is the fourteenth most common daily conversational development, this decade,' he sez to the girl alongside.

'excuse me?'

'i'm sorry, i am much misrepresented by my mouth.'

'what are you, some kind of mentalist or something?'

'enjoying yourself?'

'no. place is full of selam.'

'sellum?'

'backward males. now fuck off dad, i'm with me mates.'

'well that's it from me for tonite my lovelies. remember, the music continues til late late late so don't you go dashing off until you're certain she'll let you in to her panties. *nos da* all, ta ra & whatever he promises, make sure you use a johnny. one that's not reached its expiry date....'

lady takes her applause & rushes backstage. takes a seat & a spliff. undresses, cleanses, brushes her wig. slips into something a little less stage & out to the club. asks a member of staff to bring a large dark & stormy to her table. she settles with a well-kept male, late forties, slim, heterosexual-looking she thinks, whatever that is. they escape, safe behind their table, safe in the comfortable knowledge of their ongoing situation & watch the escapades of the drunk, the drugged, the horny, the in love. he is charming but married. the white band on his finger offers contrast to the teabag tan. aristo walks past, clocks the encounter & catches her eye. seconds stretch with the silence of so much unuttered & then he sez: 'i fucking hates that bastard aristo. he should be taken down a back alley & beaten to a throbbing pulp.'

'should i be excited by that?' she asks.

'no. you should not.'

she turns to the dance floor. watches, tries not to listen. the dj leaps from *oops outside your head* to *the macarena*. gangs of girls loop & move caterpillar-like across the spills. all double chins & treble vodkas. the middle-aged spread in spangly tops, sequins & glitter. mothers & daughters grabbing at arse & singing along with 'heyyyyyy heyyy baybee, OOH! AAH! i wanna know ow-ow-ow ow-ow-ow who ya father was!'

she's getting bored of this. tired of this. too old for this. so many nites in dodgy niteclubs pretending to enjoy herself; entertaining office workers, housing estate covens & miserable bar staff. there's only so many times in one life you can smile while watching dipshits dance *the locomotion*. this 'city full of characters' – ha, just strength in numbers, a place where the weird fuckers go to stop standing out.

lady eyes a girl in red, up at the bar, her dyed black hair so perfectly behaved but her tits like a bag of cats. the girl shoves a hand down her vest-top & shuffles her breasts, turns back to the bar only when she's comfy again. thinks no one saw her but she's been sized up. too much body on not enough legs. but still, a pin-striped dyke makes her move. she's had a lot worse. offers advice & support with the cleavage debate. the girl is intrigued. experimental lesbian involvement gets hinted at & agreed upon. 'wait. i should just tell me mates.' nobody knows if she will return to the dyke, not even herself.

calm now, he tries to drag lady's attention back to the booth: 'nice ring.'

'bit forward.'

'on your finger.'

'you don't hang around.'

'i mean the jewel.'

'ah, my rock. it's a yellow diamond.'

'worth a bit.'

'yes it is, worth a lot to me. created from the ashes of an ex-lover. he was a lovely man. a beautiful man. seemed fitting to dress with my finger in his ring.'

'how did he die?'

'smoking. we warned him enough times. but then he didn't realise that *smokin'* was the name of the articulated lorry driven by the hirsute iranian boyfriend of that young lad he was banging on the side. beat him up then reversed over his pride & joy. surprised you didn't hear of it, in builth wells it was; in all the local papers & some of the nationals. splashed over the front page & splattered over the tarmac. vertebrae popped through the skin on his back. the women in the little chef went ballistic. but that iranian bastard would never have been caught if it wasn't for the forty or so afghan refugees in the back of his lorry. frozen they were, poor dabs. them & the condemned carcasses hanging & banging. they caught him & he got deported. they got defrosted, then got deported. but the meat was never found. story of my life: all bun & no sausage. still, you could say he sacrificed his family jewels so i could wear one on my finger. & you can't turn your nose up at that kind of love.'

    '*did* you love him?'

    'yes.'

    'was he good in bed?'

    'yes. but his dick was such a piddling thing.'

    aristo reaches the men's. only two cubicles & the locks long removed. the nearest plays host to sean the porn, shoplifter to the stars & coke entrepreneur. by coke he means coke. rents a temporary space which serves as business address & places an order. expecting a delivery of x thousands cans. him & the stock will be gone the day after, as quick as a 7-up burp. they will want to know who ripped them off, an untraceable email will say 'sssch, you know who'. he is discussing distribution with the edinburgh-bred vietnamese boat-boy commonly referred to by all & sundry from monday to sunday as och aye the noodle, on account of him always out on his bike delivering, either him or hong kong tony, delivering from the chinese kitchens of clifton street to the friday nite *friends*-watching crowd. & because he's from scotland. they are discussing & smoking. creating a subsidiary to their late nite rizla delivery offshoot. they have plans & are keen.

aristo notes the collusion. the other cubicle hosts text sex
& blow jobs – texting his boyfriend to come join him. at
the urinals two men hold each other's cocks & piss all
over the tiling. the 'red ring' brand hand drier is fitting &
– surprisingly – working. nobody washes their hands.
aristo is pissed off. not a dry surface in sight, no place for
snorting.

lady & her man are pulling a caper outa here. he
doesn't want to see aristo again; she thinks even an ageing
venus with a penis needs her beauty sleep. & a damn good
seeing to.

she will wake in the morning to a bed stinking of
rough sex & rum with no idea of the day ahead, but she
knows he will leave early. by the time she wakes he'll be
home with his wife & kids. his wife will never know who
he is. his mouth full of good words treated badly. the
mattress still warm & shaped by his bones, lady will wake
alone on an edge of bed more reminiscent of a bedwetter's
share. get up for a breakfast of bensons & benylin, the
ironing, the mending. these costumes don't repair
themselves. her face is falling, her waist is spreading,
bursting the stitching, but she will smile. fuelled by the
thought of her dress on the chair a few hours previous, a
man on his knees, keen to please, careful with his teeth &
wanting her inside him.

but you gota watch who you invite. make sure you
lock up at nite. fucking, to quote the man, can be a pain in
the arse. a fucking relationship, a relationship where fuck
is the drive, or just killing time? the inevitable emotional
responses. weighing them up, sussing the lie of the land.

burning up energy, filling up spaces, mapping the geography, building bridges, logging the gradients, minefields & quagmires. the sewers under the city, the multi-storeys, the penthouse suites & back alleys, the arsenals & baby food factories, the carpet burns & carpet bombing, the shock & awe, the falling, the watching them fall, the making them mine, the making them want me want me want me, digging for your value in someone else's pants, it fucks up all life. but a good shag, noisy & fun, making love, warming & pleasing those cwtsh spots & glory holes, bouncing & giggling & grunting & moaning & juicing the grind. freeing the mind. sex forgives a lot of things, for a while. *chupa mi pena*, baby.

Messages

Glenda Beagan

Beyond concepts, this cedar tree is simply and perfectly itself.

Today I'm seeing it for the last time. After two years of false starts and rumours, Highbrake is finally closing. On Monday, staff and residents will bundle into cars, making a small and poignant convoy as they drive just a few miles down the road to the new purpose-built unit. It stands in the same grounds as a day centre and a clinic. No cedars there.

I just hope Sean won't be any trouble. He told me a while back that on the day Highbrake closed for good, he'd set off on his own and no one would be able to stop him. No one would ever find out where he'd gone either. The idea pleased him. He sat back in his chair, his hands clasped behind his head, and he looked downright smug. I saw him as a Dick Whittington figure trudging down a country lane with all his belongings tied up in a spotted scarf slung on a stick. Ridiculous, that. Sean would never go anywhere without all his atlases and all his maps, and he'd need a supermarket trolley to carry them.

'You don't actually think we'd just let him disappear into the blue yonder, do you?' Dr Hansen looked at me severely; puzzled it seemed, even offended.

'But how can you stop him if he's not on a section?' I asked. 'He knows his rights, and he's here voluntarily.'

'Only theoretically,' he said.

But the story begins twenty-two years ago. Sean was seven. I was nine. Our mother had been admitted to Highbrake the day before and here we were, visiting. It was bright October. Here was Sean, busily filling his pockets with conkers under the big horse chestnut tree. Here was I, on the same spot exactly that I'm standing now, across the car park and a piece of thin grass, falling under the protective spell of the cedar tree. I had never seen such a tree. I looked up into its silence and stillness. I did not know what the word symmetry meant but I was responding to its meaning nonetheless, as I stood below in its calm shadow and saw how its branches echoed each other on each side of the great furrowed trunk. It seemed to me that this trunk, its solidity, the sequence of strong patterns on its bark, its sheer hugeness, was somehow all part of a message I could not understand. But that didn't matter. On one level, a level without words, I understood that message. I think I fell in love with the cedar tree.

This was the first time our mother had been admitted

to Highbrake, but it was not as if she'd suddenly become ill. When you're a kid you take what's happening around you as normal, and for us it was normal to have a mother who spent most of her time in bed; hardly speaking to us, crying sometimes, making a soft low keening sound like a cat that's been trapped in a shed. Sometimes she'd be different: warm, funny, telling us stories, laughing uproariously at her own jokes, buying us expensive presents she couldn't afford, talking very fast and ever faster; flirting with the milkman, the postman, and once, memorably, shocking two fresh-faced earnest young Mormons who'd turned up on the doorstep to convert her. They couldn't get away fast enough.

After the laughter and the expansiveness, which we'd come to dread, came the next, ultimately terrifying stage, as she herself became terrified. Of everything. Of us. Of our patient, well-meaning father. Of people passing the house. People she knew. People she didn't. Of a twig tapping on the window. Of a starling on the coalhouse roof. Of the sound of the refrigerator: its low hum and the hidden message in it.

Messages. It seemed to me living was all about messages.

But I was the nervous one, wasn't I, the one who was highly strung. Sean was a lad – a real lad – and seemingly uncomplicated. He was fine, surely. No worries there. Sporty, physical, well co-ordinated, spontaneous. Not a bit shy. If anyone was fated to inherit my mother's mental problems it was bound to be me. As the years went by I took this for granted. My mother heard messages in the hum of the fridge, didn't she? I sensed them all around me. But I realise now that there was a crucial difference. My mother's messages came in words. She understood them all too well: consequently she never shared them with us. In her way, I'm sure, she was trying to protect us from them, those terrible messages that crushed her with the knowledge in them. My messages did not come in words. I didn't even begin to understand them. I didn't even try. But they were benign, I think, my messages.

Beyond concepts, the cedar tree is simply and perfectly itself.

We called them, retrospectively, The Troubles. Funny that, when you consider how our lives had never been without trouble of some kind. Still, the problems with Sean were new, and shocking. So totally unexpected. He went from an easy going eleven-year-old to a paranoid and violent twelve-year-old. It was as if someone had flipped a switch. Where does it start? Exactly? How do I pinpoint the change? Well, it surely must have begun with moving to the High School. He hated it. He'd moved from a tiny rural school which was like an extended family, to a huge impersonal monster of bustle and noise. In the third week he decided he'd had enough. He wouldn't go. More than that, he wouldn't get out of bed, and heaven knows he'd had years of exposure to that particular problem-solver. Not that it solves any problems at all. In the end.

My father had already left for work. It was up to me and my mother to attempt to get Sean off to school. It was hopeless. We managed to roll him out of bed but he lay rigid and immobile on the floor. We tried to get him dressed: pulling off his pyjamas with great difficulty, trying to ease on his clothes, lifting his arms, lifting his legs. My mother started to cry tears of rage and helplessness. Meanwhile Sean just lay there, not condescending to struggle with us, just opting out altogether. I'm sure he already had recourse to his own world, his own private mental structure, the place he would eventually live in, inaccessible to all of us. But not quite yet. Now came the long months of intervention: social workers, a child psychiatrist. He did start going to school again, but only to register in the morning and then disappear. He'd hang round town for a while, then make his way home over the fields. He sank his school bag and his books in a ditch, arriving back in the afternoon, muddy and bedraggled. He looked different. He'd grown so fast, yes, but this was something else. He had a wild look, his always-dark eyes black now, the pupils so dilated. But there was one day I'd never forget. The day that changed everything.

It was a day in early May, summer suddenly following a wet spring. I remember the mud of the path slick under our feet, the white shine and glisten of wild garlic in the wood, that oniony smell sharp on the air. And I remember the fear. What he'd told me, I didn't believe he'd done, but I was afraid of the fact that he seemed to really think he'd done it. I felt already that this wasn't just macabre make-believe, that somehow things had already gone beyond a line, a boundary, separating the difficult but still just about ordinary from the dangerously crazy. I was going to prove to him that it wasn't how he thought, clinging to the idea that you can change someone else's thoughts by producing contradictory evidence. I was being so utterly reasonable. What a fool I was. But how could I know, then, that by definition a delusion is an unreasonable idea that no amount of reasoning can shift.

He told me that he'd stampeded a herd of cows into the river. That they were all in calf and that one of the cows had panicked and had fallen and was lying in the river and was going to drown. That it was in the process of giving birth and the calf was going to drown too. His words came out in a stampede of their own. I looked at him. This wasn't a wind-up. He really believed it. And it was up to me to prove to him that it wasn't true.

We went down the path to the Mound: a favourite place for children to play, the spot which had once boasted a Norman motte and bailey castle. There was the river, as quiet and peaceful as I'd expected it to be, with Friesians grazing contentedly on the far bank.

I turned to him. 'There you are, Sean,' I said. 'Everything's all right.'

'Oh no, it's not,' he said. 'You're like all the others. You're all the same.'

He looked at me with what I can only describe as sheer malevolence. But it was desperation, really. He lashed out at me, hitting me, then kicking wildly. I put my arms up to protect my face.

'I want more,' he said. 'More. More.'

'More what?' I said, trying to avoid the worst of the onslaught, still trying to be reasonable: the sensible big sister, the troubled little brother. I wanted so much to make this right. Whatever it was he wanted I'd have got it for him. I'd have done anything.

'I hate all of you. All of you. You – none of you – know anything. You're all so fucking stupid.'

His rage was terrifying. His blows and kicks got fiercer, wilder. Instinctively I knew I mustn't fall, that I had to stay on my feet. And then I saw two people coming towards us across the field. A man and a woman, middle-aged. Wearing cagoules and walking boots. History types, we called them.

'Stop it, Sean,' I said. 'Look, there's people coming. You've got to stop it.'

And he did.

I didn't tell my parents. I kept my bruises to myself. Quiet days followed, and then he said to me, sheepishly, 'I've been round the bend; I was round the bend, wasn't I, Shona?'

'You're all right now,' I said.

But he wasn't.

I could catalogue Sean's downward spiral. I won't. I don't think I could bear to. Suffice to say that the next few years were like living in a horror film. It was nightmarish and it was pitiful. Hope can actually be very cruel. There were times when he was more – well – normal, but they were short-lived. The one thing I can't understand is that the medical powers-that-be insisted on calling it behavioural problems. We who lived with him knew it was more, and worse, than that. There were so many psychotic episodes, we lost count. Once two young policemen turned up,

called by our next-door neighbours, following one of
Sean's more public demonstrations. He'd got on the
garage roof and from there, armed with the prop for the
washing line he managed to break all the windows at the
back of the house.

'Is he schizophrenic?' one of the policemen asked. But
he'd seen the worst of it. The doctors never did. Sean was
usually able to give a brief good impression.

A few weeks after his eighteenth birthday, he was
finally diagnosed. Over a period of nearly six hellish years
he'd never been given so much as a single Valium.

I've been thinking about the whole concept of family.
What exactly is a family? It's not just a collection of
people who live under the same roof. It's an energy system
and sometimes that system goes wrong. Some sort of
pathological energy focuses on one person; expresses itself
through one person. For years, for us, this person had been
my mother. Then, following her first stay at Highbrake,
when, at last she was medicated and monitored, her
mood changes stabilizing, all that bad energy had to find
someone else to inhabit. That person was Sean. I know
there's nothing scientific about this, and I know it could
probably all be explained away as a matter of faulty group
dynamics. I still cling to this idea of interconnected energy
patterns, though. For me it makes some sort of sense.

There's a reason for all this introspection, this attempt
to disentangle our history. You might imagine that when
your mother's a manic depressive and your brother's a
chronic schizophrenic, well, you might just come to the

conclusion that it would be wise not to have children yourself.

I decided I would never have children. When I got married, James accepted this and understood. But there's a world of difference between deciding not to have children in the abstract, and actually terminating a pregnancy when despite all your precautions – somehow – pregnant is what you have become. Perhaps I was just a fatalist at heart. Perhaps this was meant to be.

James tried to put it in perspective: 'You're all right, aren't you?' he said.

What he meant was that I was adequately sane. And what he was implying was that a child of mine would not necessarily become mentally ill; that it wasn't inevitable.

'It's still a risk,' I said.

He looked at me. 'It's a risk every time you step out the front door.'

Why was Sean so ill, when I was OK? Was it just the luck of the genetic draw? There were so many questions and there were no satisfactory answers to any of them, as far as I could see. I'd thought for a time that perhaps it was something to do with my being so much a plodder. Sean had had such flair. Charisma, if you like. He stood out. He was different. Me: I plodded along, never drawing attention to myself, working hard at school because it gave me a kind of security when I needed all the security I could get. But I'd always dreamed that there was a place somewhere for Sean. A special place, an ideal environment where he'd prosper and thrive, where in order to preserve his essential self he wouldn't have to be psychotic. Or was that just a romantic evasion of what schizophrenia really was?

I'd watched a documentary once about some rare, and – it has to be said – rather stupid flightless parrots in New Zealand. Conservationists got some eggs incubated and reared the chicks by hand and then they went up in a helicopter with them to some remote island, all misty and forested. The young parrots were fitted with microchips so their whereabouts could be traced. All this time and trouble for a few peculiar birds that were really blips on the great progressive journey of evolution. (That was irony by the way!) But I'd found the film moving, I have to admit. There was something strangely lovable about these slow green creatures with their funny stubby wings and their strange feathers, overlapping semi-circles, the shape of fish scales. I wished them well in their new home, wishing at the same time that something similar could be done for Sean. Perhaps he could be a shaman in a tribal society somewhere. Perhaps on a conveniently Earth-like planet in another galaxy he could come into his own. Then I realised I was still putting my younger brother on a pedestal. It wasn't enough for him just to be well. He had to be special, too. Why did I still think like this? Perhaps because he was frozen at puberty: had never developed from the disturbed twelve-year-old whose desires were too extreme, too all-engulfing and unfathomable to ever be realised, whose imagination was turned inside out and upside down by its own unregulated power.

And now I was about to let something happen. James was very reassuring but I knew, nonetheless, that I was about to take the greatest risk of my life.

I knew the child I was expecting was a girl. And I knew what we would call her. Rebecca. Becky. I hope love will be enough.

I was very glad to go to work today, to be able to get stuck in to invoices and bills of sale, orders for baling wire and corrugated sheeting. Today was the day of the move. Even on Saturday Sean had still been in denial about the whole thing. I'd said something suitably bland about the new place, how nice it was with its en-suite rooms etc. He just looked at me with the cold, distant expression that tells you the subject is closed.

Once I got back home today my curiosity and apprehension got the better of me, and I just had to phone to find out if everything had gone according to plan. I wanted to make sure he really was safely transplanted in his new abode.

'Everything's gone very smoothly,' said Angela. 'Sean's been fine. All along he simply hadn't wanted to know, even when all the other residents went to look round the place. This morning, though, he was ready first thing, with all his maps and atlases in bags and boxes by the door.'

'He'd want to make sure none of them got left behind,' I said.

'They've all been safely delivered,' she said. 'It's a funny thing I've noticed before with other residents. Once they're sectioned, it seems to calm them. Gives them a feeling of security.'

'What?' I asked, incredulously. 'You mean he's been sectioned? When?'

'It must be a month, five weeks ago. A Section 3. That's for six months....'

I felt like saying, 'thank you, Angela. I know what a Section 3 is.' I couldn't believe this. Why hadn't I been told? For a start, wasn't it a legal requirement for the next of kin to be informed? I said all this, keeping my voice measured and even, when I was really angry. All this worry I'd had for ages, so frightened that Sean would live up to his boast that he would indeed disappear into Dr Hansen's proverbial blue yonder.

'We thought you knew,' said Angela. 'And we definitely wrote to you.'

'What made him suddenly sectionable anyway?' I asked. 'It's not as if his mental condition's deteriorated recently.' Then I heard what I was saying. Why was I coming out with all this? I was glad he'd been sectioned. It meant that even if he had decided to go walkabout they would have been empowered to bring him back. I just wish I'd known earlier, that's all.

I was giddy with relief and exhaustion and I just couldn't sleep. I lay there quietly, listening to the ebb and flow of James' breathing, wondering whether I'd give up on the idea of sleep altogether, and go downstairs to make a cup of tea. When I tried to get out of bed, though, my legs felt so desperately heavy I couldn't make the effort to move.

And then the strangest thing happened. I wonder if somehow I'd managed to half-hypnotize myself as I lay staring hard at the weave in the textured linen-effect of the curtain, the glow of the street light exposing the grid pattern of warp and weft. Whatever caused it, for the first time ever in my life I had an out of body experience.

In the no-man's-land between sleep and wake I found myself floating, literally floating along the road to Highbrake. Now that there was no reason for me to ever go along this road again, I felt a strange nostalgia for it. It was winter. The fields on the right were white with frost and on the left stood the complex of buildings we'd always known as The Main: the old Victorian mental hospital, empty for years now. As a child it had scared me stiff but I also found it fascinating. It looked to me just like a sinister French chateau in a picture book. Normally you could see the soft blue greens of the hills beyond but today a kind of radiant fog hung behind the roofs like a backdrop. The whole scene looked painted and artificial, the pinnacles and turrets silhouetted as if cut out of black cardboard. There was the central tower, denuded now of its great clock. I remembered my mother telling me how she lay sleepless at night up there in Highbrake, waiting for that icy bell to chime the hour. I felt I could hear it, a sound that was shiny and tinny and cold. But in its own way, beautiful.

I think I could have quite happily continued to float above the road for ever, but then I heard noises: wails and whispers and the ceaseless twittering of human voices. Slowly, I realised what these voices were. I was listening to the stories of all the people who had been inmates of the hospital, going right back to its earliest days, well over a hundred years ago. Their stories had never been told, and they wanted them told. I felt the pressure of a great energy of frustrated expression rising up from the old walls. They wanted me to tell their stories. They wanted the record put straight. 'How can I tell your stories,' I said. 'There are too many of you.'

There must have been thousands of them. The air was full of their aural hieroglyphics, their unbearable music. Here were their lives as lived. Here were their lives as they might have been lived. I am not an imaginative person. All I have ever allowed myself to imagine are the parallel universes I concocted for Sean. But here was a multitude of pain-lives and hope-lives combined, represented by a kind of swirling movement that kept switching itself on and off, a dance of misery, a dance of impossible alternatives.

The Babysitter

Cynan Jones

She leans back into the plush sofa. There is a pile of glossy women's magazines and a bowl of sugared almonds, pink and white.

The sofa is dark like mahogany and reddened where the leather tightens in to the hard buttons every here and there. She kicks her shoes off gently, puts up her feet on the shallow coffee table, and runs a foot along her leg, liking the way the pressure makes the stretched nylon feel against her skin. She tugs her skirt straight and holds her weight on the flat backs of her shoulders, turning the pages of the glossy magazine. She clicks the sugared almond against the inside of her teeth and looks at the photos she finds as she turns the shiny pages. A woman walking down a New York street; a woman with lips as red and loud as tulips. She looks up and fills the room with people; with handsome men and well-dressed models, and dubs a buzz of social talk across the sound of clinking glass and rich bursts of laughter. She imagines the men, catching her eye across the room. She has begun to do that on the street – look at men; not to judge them, but to see if they look back.

She flicks through the magazine and reads the quotes and snatches of the text. There's an article entitled 'I Was Used'. The plain face of a girl looks naively back at her. 'He made me feel really good and made me laugh. He seemed so nice.' 'He said I should enjoy life more.' There's a picture of him too next to his point of view. 'She didn't seem too shy to come inside.'

'I was really surprised how strong he was: he held me down quite easily.' 'Then he just went to sleep.' 'I felt so used. I'll never do a thing like that again.' The sugar coat comes off on her tongue and she feels the smooth almond. She thinks the girl is stupid and invents her own scenario, not understanding the sophistication of holding her own legs open yet. 'What about Mr___?' she thinks. He's always very kind to her.

She cracks the almond in her teeth and a log splits on the fire and she smiles at the duet and pretends she is ten years from now, her face all painted up like the woman in the picture, and the light coming off a Gucci watch she's seen in an advertisement. She leans forward and takes another sweet. (She is too young yet to feel the joy of her own pliant being, and she moves loosely and easily without thinking.) Upstairs, she hears the child wake up.

Her heels tick on the marble floor at the bottom of the stairs and ring through the empty house, and as she feels the smooth polished wood of the banister in her hand and starts to climb the stairs she wonders why a child brought up in such a house does not grow big, like a goldfish in a big pond.

The newel post is shaped like an acorn and she imagines it turning into a tree and growing through the house, with her on a swing beneath it. Looking down at her, the stern eyes of an oil painting glare and she thinks it strange to have things you never find a pleasure from.

On the landing she feels her feet sink into the thick patterned carpet and it makes her remember her shoes: her first 'grown-up' shoes. The child has started to cry.

She pushes open the door and it is heavier than she thinks. It opens slowly without a sound and the child sits up and stares at her, tiny in his loose cloth shirt.

'It's okay,' she says. 'It's okay.' (She is already a mother, and the kindness is coming into her with the turn of her hips and the filling of her breasts. Girls can be mothers before they become women.)

She sits on the bed and the child huddles into the rugs and blankets and she hears the wind come down the unlit fireplace. 'It's just the wind,' she says, and she looks at the grotesque tiles and the patterns they make as the light from the landing falls across the hearth. 'It's just the wind,' she repeats. The tiles look like they have curled up laughing mouths.

'Do you want to sleep?' she asks gently and in reply the child is still. She wants to touch his hair and wait until he sleeps, and she does not question the speed we fall in love with children. The room is too big for such a small thing.

'Read me a story,' the boy says, and the door falls open a little and makes a shadow from the curtain that looks like something else.

The book is big and heavy in her hands and it is odd because inside there's the name of a child the book belonged to once and it's a name only an old person can have. The fat cardboard of the covers is fraying at the edge and a line of children have drawn their names and coloured in the ink drawings scattered in the book. Proudly on the inside cover are the figures four to ten. The pages make her think of treasure maps and parchments.

'There once was a little girl,' she reads, 'called Little Red Riding Hood.' The hearth guffaws and the door shifts and the whole house seems to gather close, as if it wants to listen; and the big space of the house is suddenly around her. 'And once upon a time her mother bade her take some cakes and wine to Grandmama....'

She begins to grow quite nervous. As she speaks she starts to listen to herself and it is strange, like staring too long in a mirror. She sounds like a child, in her adult clothes. She wants to be downstairs again, with the facile pulp and glossy sheen of grown-up things. The smooth leather, the smooth tights, the smooth almonds and the magazines. But she's here, with another child, in the rough bedroom with the ugly tiles and the woollen sheets and the strange house huge around her. 'This delicate young thing, she'll make a tasty morsel, she'll taste much better than an old woman.' Outside a cat begins to howl and the small child's eyes go wide.

Her heart jumps and races in her chest and the cat

stops and goes away. There's a crack. 'Put the light on,' asks the boy.

Now in the light she starts again, conscious of the toys and trains that lie around the floor. 'Why! You're walking on as if you're on your way to school! Yet it's so much more fun out here in the woods.' With the light on in the room she can't see through the dark space of the window. At least, she can only see herself, reflected back. Like a child dressed for a wedding. 'What big hands you have....'

The child's eyes go closed. 'Having satisfied his appetite, the wolf lay back and went to sleep, and began to snore quite loudly.'

Carefully she stands and leaves the room, clicking off the light. She does not want to go to bed. They'll know she's more grown up if she's up when they come home. She goes downstairs and notices the fire burning low. On the coffee table lies the article, the conclusion bolded up. 'I'll never do a thing like that again.... I'll never leave the path again, and run into the forest by myself,' says Little Red Riding Hood. And the girl kicks off her grown-up shoes.

Broken Arrow

Brian Smith

He must have known what was going to happen but he walked on when it would have been safer to turn around and run. That's what I'd have done and I was half a head taller than he was. Maybe he didn't fancy the long trek down past Button Lane shops? Sensible kids from the Moss estate always chose that way home if they wanted to avoid trouble from our lot. Chancing it or just plain stupid? I couldn't decide then and I still don't know even now.

There were five of us. Jez, Michael and Tony Keady, Lamby and me. We had spent the morning making French arrows out of garden canes and carefully cut-up bits of those Spaceman cards you used to get in bubble-gum. The card flights were held in place by insulation tape. You didn't need a bow; these arrows were launched by hand and boy did they fly! A length of string with a knot at the top and a bit of know-how was all you needed to chuck a French arrow a couple of hundred yards.

By the afternoon we were bored. We'd had our competition over on the allotments – Lamby won – and were searching for something to fill the time before The Flintstones and tea.

'Moss-boy, isn't it?' said Lamby, pointing over to where this kid was heading for the hawthorn lane which separated our estate from theirs.

'He's got a nerve,' said Jez.

'Bloody cheek more like,' went Lamby.

'Needs a lesson, don't he?'

'A lesson in manners.'

Michael and Tony always seemed to echo each other those days.

'Yeah,' I said, not wanting to be left out.

'Oi, kid!' yelled Lamby. 'Piss off back the way you came, or else.' He raised his right arm, the one with the French arrow in it, and looked over at the rest of us, smirking.

I can't definitely say what I was feeling at the time. Excitement, I reckon. Bloodlust? Maybe. The other boys, my mates, seemed aggrieved. The lad was taking a liberty wasn't he? He had no right being there. This was our street. He should have gone the long way round like everyone else, shouldn't he?

The Mossy stopped for a moment, looked our way and then lifted two fingers in the V sign.

Lamby fired off his French arrow. I don't know whether he meant it to hit or miss... miss probably... but it whizzed past this kid's head and stuck in a hawthorn bush.

The Moss-boy glanced over at Lamby then plucked the arrow from where it poked out of the twigs and leaves and he snapped it over his knee. He ripped off the flights, before very deliberately dropping all the bits at his feet. All the while he stood looking at our group. Silly bugger still didn't run.

There was a sort of hush then. None of us would have dared to do that. Lamby was hard. He was our leader, cock of the estate for lads our age. He'd hammer anyone who crossed him. I'd seen him do it. Boys who had called him 'Larry' or 'lamb of God', taking the mick out of his surname with its implications of weakness. He'd pummelled me once for chanting 'Mary had a little lamb' at him one time when we'd been on opposite sides in a kick-about. And you never mentioned his mam who'd run off and left them, not unless you really fancied your chances.

The silence was broken by Michael Keady cracking his knuckles, something we'd all been eager to master that year.

'Are you gonna 'ave 'im or shall I?'

Michael had grown recently and was now the tallest and the broadest of the lot of us.

'This one's mine,' said Lamby. His lips barely moved and his eyes were wild. I knew the signs and thrilled at them.

We knew what we had to do. Me and Jez got in behind him in case he changed his mind and decided to leg it. The brothers and Lamby completed the circle.

'Pick the 'effin bits up and apologise.'

The Mossy stared at Lamby and the Keadys and then turned his head to look at me and Jez.

'Nah,' he said, 'it won't make no difference.'

Lamby's punch caught him on the side of the face just under the ear. It knocked him sideways and would have been enough to make most kids back down.

'You 'n' me,' he said, after he'd felt his cheek for any damage. 'Tell this lot to keep out of it.'

Beside me I heard Jez snort.

'We won't be needed, Mossy,' laughed Tony. 'You're in for a pastin', son.'

'All right, lads? No bother is there?'

An old bloke with a Manchester terrier had appeared from the lane. Despite the fact that it was warm he was wearing a cap and a muffler. He looked a bit puffed and he wheezed as he spoke. The dog danced and snuffled round the Mossy's legs and the old fellah took what looked like a hearing aid out of his ear.

'Lanky's winning,' he said. He took a small transistor radio from his pocket. 'One hundred and ninety-four for two. Giving the Tykes a reet thumpin' we are.' He gave us all a good looking-over. 'Marvellous things, aren't they? You can take the dog a walk and listen to the match. Me daughter give it me.'

We nodded. Aye, grand. If the kid had wanted out of it now was his chance but he just stood there like he didn't care.

'We're having a laugh with our mate from over the Moss, Mr Capper,' I said.

He had worked with my dad at Metrovick's in Trafford Park so I knew he recognised me.

'That's right,' said the kid, 'I've played football against 'em. Cricket an' all. Good mates we are.'

The old man nodded to himself then called his dog to heel in a breathy whisper.

'Aye, reet you are then. Play the game, lads, won't you?'

Silently we watched the pensioner and his scabby bitch go down the ginnel which separated his house from the one next-door. He knew the score all right.

'Garages,' said Lamby.

Organised scraps were always held there. It was out of sight of most of the houses on the estate yet formed a sort of natural arena. You could climb the drainpipes and sit on the flat roofs if you wanted a really good ringside seat or just plonk yourself against one of the green wooden doors and sit and watch.

This time we sat ourselves on the concrete like we were Apaches anticipating a knife fight.

The Moss-boy tucked his T-shirt into his jeans, shuffled his Woolworth's baseball boots and put up his fists. He seemed calm. Even a bit cocky, despite the bruise on his face starting to show.

Lamby crouched down and rushed him.

There was some way-off-the-mark swinging before the pair of them locked arms and tried to wrestle each other to the ground. The Mossy went to trip Lamby but our boy was too smart and they scuffled on the concrete, sending up clouds of dust as their feet tried to gain purchase and their legs criss-crossed, looking for advantage.

Suddenly they broke apart and without warning Lamby flung his whole body forwards. He was trying to nut him. He missed and the kid landed one right on the kisser, splitting Lamby's lip. Shit, this was even better than we'd expected.

Lamby wiped the blood away with the back of his hand. It seemed for a moment that he was going to say something but I don't think he had the breath.

'What do you reckon?' I whispered to Jez.

'What about?'

'The Mossy. Think he's got a chance?'

He wouldn't look me in the eye. Instead he gobbed in the dust.

'Dunno,' he said. 'We'll see.'

'Come on Lamby, do 'im,' yelled Michael, leaping to his feet, his face fierce with shame and disappointment.

The rest of us joined him. We were jabbing air-punches, throwing words like uppercuts, urging our boy on.

Lamby landed a couple of hits but they didn't really connect; brushed the kid's arms and shoulders is all. Both of them were bent almost double now, breathing hard and looking tired.

Just for a moment I thought they might call it quits. Shake hands or something and both walk away. You know... honours even... a draw. Daft.

They were hanging on to each other, pushing and pulling, when Lamby slipped. He knew he'd got to get up quick but he just couldn't do it... too knackered. The kid kicked him... once... twice... three times. In the belly and in the chest. It was all over, Lamby on his knees with one hand held up and looking like he was going to puke.

The winner peered down at his jeans, torn at the knee, and tried to straighten his T-shirt which had been pulled all out of shape. As he raised his head Michael clocked him right in the gob. He followed up with two more, one in the ribs and another which caught him on the nose.

'Effin' Mossy get!' spat Tony.

There was snot and blood smeared all over the Mossy's face and he started crying. I don't think it was the hurt half so much as the unfairness of it all getting to him. He'd twigged that there was no way we could let him win, even though he had.

'Scat!' ordered Michael, like he was shooting a cat.

'Yeah, and go the long way round,' added Tony, suddenly dead hard. 'Go on, get an 'effin move on.'

He made as if he was about to thump him and the kid stumbled into a painful shuffling trot. We laughed then.

I went over and helped Lamby to his feet. Jez stuck close to the Keadys. Michael took a packet of ten No. 6 from his jeans and gave one to his brother. He didn't offer one to Lamby. They lit up and Michael blew a plume of smoke in the air.

'Gave you a good kickin' didn't he? That Mossy?'

Lamby said nothing.

'Maybe you should stick to beatin' up women like your old man?'

I saw Lamby's bloodied knuckles clench but there was still no reply.

'You fought like a big tart.' He took another drag. 'Not surprising really... considering what your old girl used to get up to.' Michael paused for effect. 'Still does, probably.'

He flicked the fag away so he could be ready but there was no need.

Michael turned to Tony and Jez.

'Five card brag at ours?' he suggested.

They both nodded.

'You comin', Phil?' he asked.

I didn't even hesitate.

'Yeah, 'course.'

'Lamby?'

So, for the rest of the afternoon the five of us gambled our pennies in amongst the bikes and garden tools in the Keadys' shed and if anyone gave a thought to what had happened not one of us mentioned it.

By tea-time I was more excited by the one and a tanner I'd won at the turn of a few cards than I was by a broken arrow and a new way of looking at things.

Only on a Sunday Morning

Geoff Dunn

'I'm not made for babies, Albert.'

That's what she said to me on our wedding night.

'What was that you said, Gwyneth?'

'I said that the Good Lord in all his wisdom has told me that I was not made to bear children so you'd better have the precautions.'

'Yes,' I said, 'I've been to see Ronnie the Barber and bought some Frenchies.'

'There's no need to be so crude, Albert, but if that's what you've done you can put one on and get on with it.'

So I got on with it.

I could hear my friends laughing.

'What's it like with the Ice Maiden, Albert?'

'Remember Port Eynon?'

'And that little Girl Guide on the Gower?'

'I bet she's teaching her husband a few tricks now!'

I stop, paralysed, thinking about the little slut. Gwyneth asks if there's anything wrong, but I can't say a word.

'Get on with it, Albert,' she says. 'Don't take all night. I'm getting sore. You know I'm not made for babies.'

'Yes, Gwyneth.'

*

There's a phone on the other side of the corridor, one of those dingy grey wall-mounted things and a sign with peeling yellow sticky tape that says: 'Staff Only'.

Doctor Anna's on it now. I like her. She's got a little white coat, a stethoscope and shiny blonde hair. Look! She's just smiled at me. I really do like Doctor Anna.

My bed is just inside the ward, right next to the entrance. There shouldn't be a bed here at all really but this is where they've put me. Doctor Anna has just finished on the phone. I'll give her a little wave.

'How are you this morning, Mr Sketty?'

'Call me Albert,' I say to her.

'Are you enjoying your holiday?'

I must look puzzled, thinking about the Gower, but she goes on: 'Your holiday here, while the builders finish altering your ward upstairs.'

'Oh, my holiday.'

I'm still a bit confused but we both laugh together.

We're interrupted by Mr Llewellyn-Jones who breezes in: sharp grey suit, blue silk tie, gold pin. Now there's class for you! White-coated doctors and several nurses trail in his wake. Doctor Anna slots herself into the procession.

'What on earth are all these extra patients doing here?'

Someone attempts an explanation about the work upstairs but they're cut short.

'Worse than a damned Crimean field kitchen! Does this one really have to be stuck in the entrance like this?'

He's looking at me, granite-faced, as I try to hide under the sheets.

'Right, let's get on with it. This one's not one of mine, is he?' Mr L-J is looking at me again. I don't know which is worse, being scared stiff or disowned. I decide to make myself very small and wait until he's gone.

*

That phone has been ringing for ages. There's a frosted glass door next to it and windows you can't see through either. The door opens and this chap comes out. He is a strange-looking fellow: bald head, great big shoulders and the longest, skinniest legs you've ever seen. What makes it worse are his pyjamas. I mean, me and the boys from upstairs have all got proper ones, warm and fleecy with stripes and long trousers tied up with a cord around your waist, but he's got these shiny green silk things with shorts! If I had legs like him, I wouldn't dress like that, at least not in public.

'Oi! Nurse, Doctor, somebody; for Christ's sake answer that bloody phone will you!'

And he goes back in his little room and slams the door.

He's not from round here. I can tell by the way he speaks, a bit like that Del Boy. I'd say London. He's definitely not Swansea. I wonder what's wrong with one of his hands. I've never seen so many bandages – looks like a big white boxing glove.

A young male nurse has just answered the phone – only looks a kid, nice lad, mind, though he's a bit... well how can I put it... a bit sort of... 'girly'.

Daddy Longlegs has come out again.

'Oi! Nursey Boy! Get here quicker next time. I've paid a lot of money for private treatment and I don't expect this sort of disturbance.'

I don't think I like him.

I wish Doctor Anna was here.

*

I've been thinking about the phone. It'd be nice to ring my Gwyneth, find out how she's going on. There's a skinhead in the bed round the corner, tattoos all over him, tried to creep out in the night and phone his girlfriend but he couldn't get a dialling tone. I suppose I'll have to wait until Gwyneth can come here. The travelling isn't easy if you can't drive.

*

I'm starting to enjoy my holiday. This bed's in a lovely position. I can see and hear everything that's going on – not that I'm nosey, mind. Sometimes all the doctors gather in the corridor and discuss people. I can't understand a lot of it. Too many big words, but I'm starting to pick them up. Old Huw Price in the corner over there, he's from upstairs like me. Well, whenever they mention him their voices go all quiet and serious. Makes me think he hasn't got long, but he still keeps pestering me.

'Albert, bach, what did they say about me last night?'

I daren't let on that I don't know. He's a grumpy old sod and he'd have a dickey fit, so I tell him he's got a 'bilateral distalgesic endoscopy'.

'Is that bad, Albert bach?'

'Not as bad as the night before,' I tell him. 'I think you're on the mend.'

*

I can hear Daddy Longlegs shouting in his frosted glass palace.

'What do you mean I can't use a mobile in here? Well, get me the bloody payphone then! What do you mean it's down on Ward Two? Listen, Nursey Boy: that's bloody NHS! Has it escaped your tiny brain that I'm private? Look, it might well say 'Staff Only' but you're staff so get me a bloody line!'

He's very red-faced when he comes out, the nurse I mean. He taps away at the phone and passes the receiver to Daddy Longlegs.

'You'll get me into trouble, Mr Cromby. I'm not doing this again.'

Well, the fact is he did and I've been listening all the

time. If you want to know my opinion, I think he's a gangster. Yes, it's all there in black and white. Had his thumb cut clean off with a knife and now while they're stitching it back on, he's organizing a van load of his London mates to come down here and sort out the 'unfinished business'. If you ask me, he's a nasty bit of work.

I wonder if that nurse could get me an outside line? It would be nice to talk to Gwyneth, but I can't seem to attract his attention. Perhaps he's private, too.

*

The skinhead round the corner has just shouted: 'Look out! Pit stop!'

I don't know what he means but looking up I see a tiny nurse. She must be as old as me, no more than four foot six and wrinkled like an oak stump. She wears a huge plastic apron and rubber gloves up to her armpits.

Before I can speak, she's throwing me around like meat on a butcher's slab. My head hangs over the side of the bed as she rips the sheets away. I'm looking at her shoes, waiting for the flick knives to pop out of her toes. Then whoosh, I'm staring at the ceiling and she says: 'There you are, Mr Sketty, clean as a whistle. Who's next?'

I take comfort in the crispness of the clean sheets. My Gwyneth always had a thing about clean sheets.

*

I must have been asleep for some time. There's a nurse standing at the end of my bed. She's pretty, but in a strange sort of way, black curly hair and the most incredibly big red-brown eyes that sink into her sunset cheeks. I'm sure I've seen her before but I can't think where. I force my hand from the tightness of the new-made sheets and try to wave to her. Her eyes sink lower but she says nothing. I see the whiteness of her knuckles grasp the metal tubing of my bed. My voice chokes in my throat and it's sunset.

*

It's been busy today, really busy, must be the weekend. I've never seen so many visitors. Quite a few of them seem to know me already.

'Hello, Albert,' they say.

I give them this little wave. It's a bit like the Royals. They all wave back but no one ever stops to talk to me and yet I'm in such a commanding position.

I can't understand it.

I wonder if the Queen ever feels like me?

Whatever is keeping my Gwyneth?

*

Doctor Anna is holding my hand. I've not seen her for a while. I wonder why she's doing that?

'It's Huw,' she says.

'Huw?'

'Huw Price, over there by the window, your friend. I'm afraid he passed away last night.'

I scour my memory, find no one called Huw Price but I don't want to upset Doctor Anna, so I say: 'That's bad.'

She looks deep into my eyes, carefully pulls out my thoughts and says: 'You're not feeling yourself, today, are you, Albert?'

*

The skinhead with the tattoos has just whispered in my pillow. He says he knows how to get an outside line on the staff phone. It's zero nine. Fancy that! Just two little numbers stopping me from talking to Gwyneth. So I drop into a long, deep sleep and dream about all the things I have to tell her.

*

What the hell is this cinemascope plate-glass view doing next to my bed? I can see the whole town leading down to a sea horizon, vast and empty. Where's my little doorway full of people? What do I want with this stupid huge window? Where's Doctor Anna? She wouldn't do this to me.

Nurse Stumpy's wrinkled lips are rubbing on my ears. She's got a voice like Louis Armstrong.

'You might as well have old Huw's bed, now that he's gone, God bless him. Mr Llewellyn-Jones says you were in the way over there, but what a view you've got now, *cariad*! I did it all while you were asleep. Didn't take ten seconds! I bet you're pleased, aren't you?'

I wince at the thought and nod but my voice deserts me as it always does at times like this.

It's all going wrong. How will Gwyneth ever find me now? Where are you, Doctor Anna? Even Stumpy has gone. I feel so alone. This huge view makes me feel so small and insignificant and I've just realized something else. How ever am I going to get to the phone to dial zero nine?

*

She's at the foot of my bed again, the black-haired one with the sunset eyes. I manage to say: 'Hello.' She looks slightly askance at me, runs the tip of her tongue around her barely-parted lips and says nothing. I feel I ought to be afraid but there's something pulling me towards her. I've seen that look before. Oh yes, I feel my fingers twitch as my mind hurtles back. I can smell the wet grass, the salt in the air and I'm looking at a young girl. She still wears a blue uniform. She's standing behind a dry stone wall that has partly collapsed. There's a single strand of barbed wire across the top, supported by some crumbling, lichen-covered posts. I've left the big bell-tent where I'm camping with the Boy Scouts. I can't sleep. I've never been away from home before. It's early in the morning but the sun is bright and the shadows so long. I'm sure we are the only two awake on the whole of the Gower. She follows the boundary of the field where the Girl Guides are camping, beckoning me towards a five bar gate which hangs from its broken hinges at the bottom. She still hasn't said a word as she takes my hand and we set off for the dunes. That's how it was, I swear to you, she never said a word.

She led me into the trembling marram grass, lay down and put my hand where it had never been before. Oh, the joy and then the panic, the shuddering muscle-wrenching panic as I ran back to the camp and fell gasping into the tent.

'How did you get on then, Sketty?'

And I told them a bravado tale of sand-smeared kisses and so much more.

They all fell about laughing and said: 'Join the club, Albert! We've all been there too. Surprised it took you so long.'

I ran out. A sudden squall had blown in from nowhere and was flapping the coarse brown canvas of the tent. I looked across at the still-sleeping Guide camp and, fighting back the tears, felt raindrops the size of plums smack into my face.

*

I remember Gwyneth going into hospital. She wouldn't say what for, but she came out, all smelling of disinfectant and said: 'I told you all along, Albert. I wasn't made for babies so they've taken all the...'

'All the what?'

'All the... well, you know, Albert. All the...'

Before I could ask her if she was all right, I found myself saying: 'Good, I won't need to go to Ronnie the Barber now, will I?'

Gwyneth, rather strangely, smiled.

'You're smiling,' I said. 'Why is that?'

'Well, if having babies is out of the question for me, trying to make them will be out of the question for you, won't it?'

*

Doctor Anna is back and I'm back too, in my little bed by the doorway where I can see everything that's going on. Doctor Anna sorted that for me. What a treasure she is! She said I was suffering from 'psycho- something' distress. I must tell old Huw Price that one. Daddy Longlegs' thumb must be on the mend. He's nowhere near as bad-tempered as he was and I've not heard him make a phone call to his London friends yet, though I still don't trust the gangster.

Where's Gwyneth? She should be here by now. Doctor Anna said it was distressing for me by that big, frightening window so I'm sure she would have told me if there was anything wrong with Gwyneth. I'll sink into my soft pillow. I won't make a fuss.

*

It was after she came back from the operation that she started starching the sheets. I told her they felt like porcelain. I almost felt they would break as I folded them back to get into bed with her. I told her that though I respected the fact she couldn't have babies, it wasn't the same for men.

'I don't quite understand,' she said, 'but if you're not going to Ronnie the Barber, something will have to be done about the sheets.'

She began to love whiteness, purity; washing her hands, scrubbing them with a floor brush and bleach until they were red and raw.

For my part, I obtained a piece of plastic sheeting, as she had asked. It measured twenty inches by twenty-four, to be inserted under her buttocks, only between the hours of nine and ten on a Sunday morning, to be subsequently washed by me and dried in the airing cupboard until the following Sunday morning. I called it 'my prayer mat'.

That's how it went on. Sunday morning prayers, Monday morning put the bins out, Tuesday morning... well, does it really matter?

It didn't until one Sunday morning.

I was awake early, couldn't sleep. I woke her and told her it was time for prayers but she said she was thirsty and wanted a cup of tea. On my way to the kitchen I noticed the paper boy had already been, so I took her the Sunday paper as well as the tea and a few biscuits for good measure. As she read, I became intrigued with the football reports on the back page and trying to read the smaller print I found myself lying between her legs and...

...Well, there was this report how a goal had been scored in the last minute...

...You can imagine the rest.

She never lowered the newspaper, but long after she continued to writhe and moan beneath me. I tried to pull the paper away but she clutched it to her face with hands spread wide. I tugged at her hands but her hips lifted me up and down until she let out a scream so agonising that it left me strangling the pillow.

It was nearly half an hour before she took the paper away from her face.

'Albert,' she said. 'We must never, ever do anything like that again.'

*

She's there at the foot of my bed again, the black-haired one with the sunset eyes, running her tongue around her barely-parted lips. The blue uniform confuses me. It's not just that but memories of Gwyneth. How could she be so joyful and so tearful?

Why do I yearn for a rain-splashed Gower?

I suddenly become aware that Sunset Eyes is not looking at me but at Daddy Longlegs who is standing at the foot of my bed beside her. Their eyes meet and he beckons her towards his frosted-glass lair. I sit bolt upright on my pillow.

'Got a problem, Grandad?'

'No, no, you can take her.'

As she disappears into his private room she blows me a kiss but I pretend not to see it.

*

It's zero nine. I know it's zero nine because the skinhead told me. Stumpy has made me turn somersaults as she's changed the sheets but no matter, I still keep asking her to phone zero nine for Gwyneth.

'That's just a code. You'll need your home number, *cariad*.'

'I haven't got a code. I haven't got a number. I live here.'

The reality hits me hard but I feel so happy when Stumpy says she'll fetch Doctor Anna. Maybe she can sort something out.

*

'Albert?'

'Yes.'

'It's me, Doctor Anna.'

'Doctor Anna?'

'Yes. Gwyneth died a long time ago. You know that, don't you?'

'Do I?'

'Yes, you do, Albert.'

'Then I've got no one.'

'Yes you have, Albert. No more self pity. You've got me and a lot of other people to keep an eye on you now.'

*

And that's how it was. I ate my breakfast like a good boy, even tried to get out of bed while Stumpy changed the sheets until they promoted me back upstairs.

'Well done, Albert,' they said, 'you've made it back where you belong.'

'Yes, back on top of the world,' I said as I crawled like a rat between the sheets.

That's how it is up here. No one ever visits. The uniforms are the same but the faces are like a masked ball. Pull away the mask and you'll never find the same face. They change by the week. You'll never know whose hand is pulling away at your pyjama bottoms.

'Hello, Albert.'

'Doctor Anna!'

'Yes, I thought I'd see how you were going on.'

'Gwyneth is dead, isn't she?'

'Yes.'

The sterility of the silence is broken by a pallid student nurse.

'Have you seen this in the paper, Doctor?'

'What?'

'It's all across the middle pages, look.'

Doctor Anna sits at the foot of the bed, holding the newspaper open in front of her as I gaze at the football reports on the back page. As she reads, she lifts her feet off the floor and makes herself more comfortable. I lean forward to read the account of the matches. I don't know how it happens. I don't know why, but there's this feeling under the sheets, something I've not felt for years and years, a wonderful warm feeling and Doctor Anna is still behind the paper as I put my hand on the firmness of her thighs.

She says two words.

'Oh, Albert.'

That's all she says.

I'm not sure whether she's pleased or telling me off so I move my hand another inch under her skirt.

She holds my wrist tightly.

The young nurse walks away as Doctor Anna says how good the centre-page article is.

I move my hand another inch or two.

'Albert!'

I see the full colour picture of the goal, the despairing lunges of the defenders, the helpless outstretched arms of the keeper, the open mouths and flailing arms of the crowd and Doctor Anna is struggling as I say how sorry I am as I push my right hand between her legs. She tries to sit up but I press the paper over her face with my left hand and force her head into the pillow.

'Please Albert, please.'

'What does she want?' I ask myself. 'What do I do now?'

I find my hand tugging at the knotted cord of my pyjama bottoms as I throw back the sheets and pull her towards me. I am aware of the distant screaming of the student nurse as Doctor Anna tries to pull the newspaper from her face, cradling me between her legs, writhing, heaving.

Someone is pulling the hair at the back of my head and shouting for help but the ball is still in flight, the keeper's arms clawing futile and the mouths of the crowd all-devouring as Doctor Anna says: 'No! Oh, my God Albert, no... please... no... no... no!'

And the windows blow open as the wind lifts the curtains and the sunlight of a lifetime floods the ward.

I don't know how many of them there are.

They've pulled me off the bed onto the floor but they can't stop my body moving nor the beautiful agony in my mind as Doctor Anna looks down at me and it's endless. This feeling of warmth is endless and she keeps on looking down into my eyes and for the first time I realize I've never been so happy in all my life.

'What day is it?' I ask them, aware of a shadow as they surround me.

No one replies.

'It's not Sunday, is it?'

'No, it's not Sunday,' says Doctor Anna, straightening her hair.

'How marvellous!'

And I start to laugh and I keep on laughing as they pick me up. I'm still laughing as they put me back in my bed and draw the curtains around me.

I Learned When I Was Older

Miranda Evans

Journeying

My torn-cuff jumper and tree-climbing trousers were
grimaced off and tutted away.

Shoe-horned into sulkiness
dressed to depress
my Sunday best
hung ill-fitting
on their tom-boy frame.
Like cut-out clothes
on a paper doll
I shifted in the stiffness
while they stayed still.

Mum had stitched the name-tape into the wrong uniform. To compensate for her cola-bottle dolly and her lost baby girl.

There were two ways to get to Grandma's house on a Saturday afternoon. Both had their merits and their hazards. Mum jabbed the Jag haltingly along our back lane. Lurching, edging, puffing, sweating. I was cowed into silence by her furrowed brow in the rear-view mirror. Mum had a look which kept our fingers out of the pick 'n' mix. She learnt it from her mother, but it never quite rang true.

She needed guidance from a higher authority than the vulnerable wing mirrors. She stopped to gather her wits and call on Saint Christopher. Time slowed to a crawl to join us. Pedestrians hovered uncertainly.

The car's voluptuous curves threatened to swell with her increasing heartbeat. Rusty iron down-pipes struggled to resist the impish urge to spring from the church-hall wall. Broken glass antagonised the tyres. Pebble-dash leered at us.

Wincingly close to the flawless metallic paintwork, ('silver-blue', Dad called it) Mattie and Bryn's corrugated cottage inched past. A closer fit than cotton wool in a bottle-neck of Junior Disprins. We held our breath and waited for the twisting screech.

I traced upholstery stitching with unnatural fascination. Dad would have shrunk involuntarily from the obstacles. Now piling himself discreetly against the passenger door, now crowding-out the gear-stick.

238

Eyes in neutral.
Wisely silent.
Saying nothing under torture.

He said she'd let go of the wheel once, panicked when she was learning, in the face of an oncoming tractor. She loved speed, but couldn't manoeuvre.

'You've got my lead foot,' she told her middle boy through lowered eyebrows. Almost conspiratorially. Said with a kind of pride.

Mum swung her ship, nose-dipped into the unsuspecting traffic.

Other times, when her nerves weren't up to driving, we went on the bus. She told me I took my imaginary friend with me; I expect for moral support. My mother's driving was scary, but her mother was another matter.

There was the consolation of the bus journey to enjoy first, though. It offered opportunities for tiny tests of bravery and skill, all with a safety net. There were plenty of seats to choose from besides the one by my mother. So long as I didn't go too near the back where the big boys smoked and swore.

I instinctively knew the ridicule my furry earflaps and chinstrap would provoke. My bobble tempted torment. My brothers had inadvertently taught me caution.

I could improve my judgement and timing. I showed off my knowledge of local geography, appearing worldly-wise by anticipating our stop. I demonstrated my agility, by wobbling wrong-footed to the front of the bus, pinballing into each seat that I passed.

My feigned nonchalance was knocked out of me by the rough kids who flew forward with the alarming speed of gypos on the waltzers. I grazed my shins on apple-boxed groceries filled with caulis cherished in newsprint smelling of soap powder. I refused to be seen wincing.

Never mind. Sinfully aware of my charms, I could air my good manners, making old ladies coo by daring to thank the driver. Unaided, I stubbornly tackled the stairs. Small steps to independence and the downfall of pride.

The only time as a child that I ever saw my mother cry was when I told her I wanted to go on the bus on my own.

We'd reached number 12. Peopled by the now long-dead. The adrenaline rush of journeying was over. Time for me to pipe down.

Inside

The formidable beloved matriarch drew us in. Not that she ever answered the door – the men of her house leapt to that duty. Everybody came to Granny, and Granny visited no one. She never saw a need to leave the house. She sent out a fleet of sea-faring sons to sail oceans, skim continents and bring back the world loyally to her lap with tales of their travels and dragon-laced teapots.

I imagine her now as a stiff 1930's Hollywood Elizabeth the First receiving her envoys returning from foreign lands and New Worlds. But she wasn't skinny and pinched like a movie regent, no: she was solid, meaty, neatly girdled, planted firmly on her chair, her hand resting purposefully on the top of her stick. Her walking aid, it betrayed no whiff of weakness, it was part of her regalia.

It was her bearing and manner that reminded me of Elizabeth. Would she bestow you with honours or chop off your head? You didn't mess with Granny. Now it was our turn to deliver respect and news from her provinces. Unlike my heroically-dimensioned nautical uncles, we'd only come up from town on the bus. I never felt quite worthy of an audience.

Time and repetitive action burnished the details of this place into my bones. It sank heavily through my skin and entered my bloodstream. With resignation, I knew what to expect.

Here, bricks and mortar behaved themselves and the room would be blinded by decent nets. Joey would be fidgeting himself featherless behind bars. Time, as always, would be cased reverently within the glass dome. China dogs, transfixed by the moment of promise would be forever aching for the nod to leap upwards:

TO BE UNSYMMETRICAL!

Standing on the doorstep crammed into my white lacy Pex Tights for Girls, the dogs had my sympathy.

'Here she is, that Long One,' Granny would say from her throne as she observed my mother's elegant, considered approach to the house. Aware that she was being watched.

We were on the threshold of a place where disconcertingly, my mother wasn't at the top of the pecking order. I felt the bump of the knock-on effect and sought out diversions to hide me from judgement. The best of these was Joe. He was trying to learn the way to behave in this house too.

Mum said he was like Clark Gable, but I just saw George Best. I wanted his attention, but his eyes just glided past me. They were on the higher plane of budgie cage and *Tit-Bits*.

A constant tot of whiskey filled a tiny glass in one hand, the smoke from a rollie plumed, slow-motion, like ink in water from the other. He performed communion with a silver box of papers and an ashtray made of brass.

Timeless and iconic, his arms rested lightly on the antimacassars like the outstretched arms of Jesus. I ate my buttered Rich Tea biscuits and was thankful. I was thankful for the stimulus. I eked out the small experience. I picked hard, tiny gems of coal from my knees and then like fleas from the red hearth rug.

My furry collar itched. They know not what they do.

Radio Luxembourg whispered at his right ear from the top of the calcifying china cabinet as he watched silent wrestling on the TV screen. Giant Haystacks struggled murkily in his gold-fish bowl distortion. The screen was fifteen inches thick.

Miranda Evans

None of the signals got through.

All of the signals got through.

TV, radio, *Tit-Bits*, budgie,
quarter-hour clock-chimes, knock-knock scarper,
snot-nosed five-a-side, bus-stop diesel thrum,
china chinks,
kettle whistle,
granny babble,
poker-rattle,
even Joey's cuttle-fish piano.

The air was thick with information and messages seen
and unseen, coal-smoke and tea-steam. Over-sensitised,
Joe tried to tune out scratching niece, hacking Grandpa,
hairsprayed sisters. I was trying to tune myself out of the
picture, and see and hear everything unobserved by
Granny's brow-hooded disapproval. Anxious little shoreline
crab, I shovelled myself under.

   At first, I thought Joe had mastered the good manners
required to wait patiently for time to pass. We were both
waiting for time to pass; I was still learning to be patient.
My time was bus-timetable small-scale. His was a World
Without End, Amen.

   I almost dared to hope for a secret unspoken solidarity
with Joe, but was afraid that even thinking this would
evaporate the possibility. It was a thought as wished for but
as futile as trying to grasp the fluid rainbow magic of a
floating soap-bubble. Every week he was here, as reliably

as my guinea pig was always in its hutch, yet totally unreachable. Still I felt a connection; that he and I were almost in the same place.

But Joe's place
was a private haven elusive as a waking dream.
My place
was to be seen and not heard.

If anyone had asked me, my place was at home in front of Dr Who with a packet of Smoky Bacon, tricked into playing silent statues by my father all through the football results. At Granny's, the television exploded into seismic sound. Ballpoints sank through paper grids into the plump tablecloth beneath with the force of concentration. I had to become more invisible than ever. Joe remained unaltered.

The parlour clocks were out of step.
The gold balls in the domed clock
switched seamlessly,
silently
endlessly
clockwise, anti-clockwise, clockwise.

His Mona Lisa eyes blinked and smilingly slid around the room, but never stopped at me.
Everything here needed to escape. Joe already had. The room itself wanted to romp around the dog-shit green outside, with the kids with brown teeth.
Yet in his knitted zip-up cardi Joe was untouchable.

Miranda Evans

Centered like a Buddha, shielded by a veil of Golden
Virginia. Secret vinegar drinker. Poised and languid in his
brass-studded arm chair, he threw grenades at women and
children. The most handsome man I had ever seen.

My schizophrenic uncle Joe was smiling at a private joke.

Free-floating, fascinating captive. Compelling viewing for a
six-year-old. His deliberate ease was an unsustainable
avoidance, a temporary release. A Dad's Army helmet to
the shell bursts. Even so it required great force of will,
faith, the imagination of a magician. But Joe could turn
water into wine. He had told my mother so. For his next
trick, when he finally lost his patience, he decided to
control time.

Clean slippered, he slit his wrists.

Outside

Sing-song icecream chimes dared me to go outside. Kids I
knew but didn't play with pestered at the door. Awkward
and untrusting, I was winkled out for skipping. Or thumping.

My hateful dolly clothes whispered victim.

Stay away from the Green where they
tackled dirty, threw stones, had fleas, twisted arms,
grew warts and chinese burnt you

or lurking on the bus-stop roof
gobbed on people.

My brother isn't bigger than your brother,
but he's trickier,
he's nippier,
he's faster on his feet.
Skinny-rib Knievel Kid
will wind you
and spin you
and knock you for six

YES!
Our nifty lightweight
will wrong-foot you and
LEAVE YOU STUPID!
And me cheering.

To myself.
Well I was hardly going to show him I was proud.

Sometimes, I got invited in.

His teeth and spit were in my face. More scary than the
yo-yo Jack Russell that had made me scream. He told me to
effing shut up. And his mum was in the kitchen. My
ringlets were glaring and I reddened under my bobble.
    The girl from school was surprised that I was shocked.
I was shocked that she was surprised. Held aloft, my ice
cream wafer sandwich dribbled down my arm. I was spoilt.

Granny, Ma Maguire, knew how to stand up for herself. She'd had to. She had brought up three families of seven children. She had scrubbed for twenty-one. She wasn't averse to telling you. And who can blame her?

As Kitty Brennan, the eldest of seven siblings, she had brought them up herself when her mother died. Married at seventeen, her husband was twenty years older. He was my real grandad, but TB left her with her second seven to feed.

Granny kept his photo edged with silver. Ten years of doorstep scrubbing and laundry washing later, his silent matinee idol looks were finally replaced by Pa Maguire. My mother slid her dashing sailor hero back into the frame he'd never left. She was only three when he had died, she'd never really known him.

She later brought him back to life.

Treasured in oval sepia tone, travelling through time, my eldest brother spiralled mustachioed from the frame. Her first surviving child. Her favourite, no wonder.

Jealousy, behind the spinning clocks, was depicted as top cat and underdog.

Cushioned in the arms of an elegant lady,
the long-haired kitty looked down.
The satin-bowed Collie looked up.

Girls are cats and boys are dogs.

Aren't they?

The tomboy girl and the gentle boy beg to differ.

Both groomed pets were equally well cared for and loved. In a way that Granny had never had resources for. My careful presentation seemed to rile her. It had the opposite effect to that intended. She viewed my mother's efforts sideways, head tilted backwards: with distaste? I was spoiled.

As everyone revolved around Granny, she had no need to leave the house, not even to do the shopping. She had plenty of children and grandchildren at her command for that. So it was a truly unheard-of event that following a brainstorm, she decided to go to town.

The queen bee waited at a bus-stop with her entourage. A boy from her youth paused in passing. No greeting, though he'd not seen her for decades.

Just:
your Kathleen, your daughters.
(His gaze swung around at her ladies-in-waiting.)

Pause...

all fine-looking women.

Then...

not a patch on their mother, no match at all.

Ma Maguire was suspicious of flattery. Kitty Brennan allowed herself a smile.

248

Miranda Evans

Respite

The outside toilet was reached by a walk through the kitchen, which at any other time was a forbidden trap of feet I would get under and things that cut and burnt.

The plastic bowl in the metal sink sat wedged beneath rubber fittings on the taps. Carrot-orange rubber fittings, faded and gone warty; what were they for? The gingham was wipe-clean, covered in crumbs of holy hot-cross buns, sugar and ants. Cold smell of pantry; damp; marrowfat cardboard and Lux flakes, cheap plastic slap of coloured strips, like my flip-flops at home. Why not a door?

A single metal tablespoon rocked in the wooden table drawer. An open pint of milk warmed in a cold-water pan.

Bubbly oval glass in the doors of a cupboard the colour of a church-hall tea-cup. How many colours had it been? A history of chips belied its spring-cleans. Down through the strata to an age where Ma Maguire had been more than just handsome.

I loved the woolly cosy for its bands of knitted colour. A novelty we didn't have at home. I pushed my fingers in the pom as it guarded the Glengettie. I hesitated in a soundless appeal to be accompanied to the loo, too ashamed to admit that I was scared. It had no light and was full of spiders.

Shaped from the darkness and blended to the black, hairy backs hung lurking. Suspended by sorcery, a thickening tracery first invisible, then opaque, took the weight of their filthy stares – a point of dirty heat behind my shoulder. Hiding from the split and dusty light,

squatted and heaving, the dark corners shifted slightly. I
didn't want my eyes to adjust to the light.

Grandpa coughed and held the door. I couldn't reach
the latch. I couldn't touch the seat. Caught between two
worlds, I hovered in discomfort. I got it over with as fast
as I could in the dark.

I preferred Grandpa. I could see his slippers through
the gap below the door. I'd rather wet myself than ask
Granny. She scowled and had a stick. Imagine weeing on
her crocheted cushions. I did.

Sometimes Mum came in with me, seeking refuge in a
cigarette. One of many.

Hunting in her handbag past hanky and hairpin treasures.
Leafing over saints and parish news.
A rosary to worry later.
Mintoes and glucose, a ribbon for my hair.
Scuffed silver stub of Fry's Chocolate Cream.
Gathering fluff.
Reaching past the childproof rattle
for her saviour and the match with which to burn him.
You will say 20 Embassy Number Six
and 40 Gold Leaf as your penance.

Holy smoke.

By the ungratefulness of God, with the faith of an angel,
my mother was afraid of everything she needed;

Miranda Evans

Cigarettes, Granny, religion and love.

Mum warmed the seat for me.
Grandpa drowned the spiders for me.
We counted as they floated in the tin bath out the back.
Legs limp and lovely as my long hair in a swimming pool,
last week's ones had sunk,
I noticed smugly.
Broad and black,
Granny never came outside.

The sun had strained to breach the nets of the smoky, tea-stained room, it had struggled limply through milky fug to blind the TV screen opaque. Here with Grandpa, it finally filled its lungs, expanded wide and lit up the colour in welcome.

The path was joyfully child-sized; made for me, overhung with sweet-peas and the vague flight of bumble-bees. Buddleia lifted with Cabbage Whites. My head swam with whiskered Sweet William. It was better to be outside with Grandpa. His chin was bristly silver and he never wore his teeth. I understood no word of his whistling toothless Irish accent, but I knew just what he meant.

Grandpa meant strawberries,
dusty from under the netting,
deliciously,
illictly,
GRANNY-FREE!

Pitted and shaped like his broken nose. He was soft-hearted and no oil-painting.

I collected empty snail shells when Grandpa disappeared into the coal shed. Perfect, tiny baby snail, baby's nail translucent. A tissue-thin delicacy finer than china. I marvelled at their preciousness, I held them to the light, I counted them out with greed.

So easily, wickedly,
CRUSHED
under my cruel patent t-bar,
or minced
between my fingers.

Fierce bud of defiance, I exercised my small powers with a shiny and demented glee. Beyond the boundaries of Granny's domain, I was now a citizen of Grandpa's gentle realm. Let off the leash, I could choose to crush the shells or prize them. Joe's escape was to spin his own Alhambra Palace from radio waves and tobacco shreds. My mother hermit-crabbed the coal-shed.

They prodded her back out with electricity. Grandpa saw it broken-hearted, thumbing through the horses.

I'd rather be in control than in the shed. Mum had hid in there when people called, I learned when I was older.

Hooked with a kind of crawling horror, I saw that the flowers were squashy with beaded blackfly.

Visitors

Auntie Biddy, meanwhile, plush cheeked and truly beautiful, shone from the frame that held her, onto other visitors who called. She bestowed a velvet smile from way too high to reach. A single string of pearls glowed around her simple roll-neck. A testament to Ma Maguire's faded Kitty Brennan days.

My cousin Kevin was better than Feargal Sharkey's. He didn't have a sheepskin jacket that cost a packet. His was made of denim. He was long-haired and lovely, like his silky collie bitch. Devoted to his dog, we saw them pass the Green unchallenged, a class act. Shrouded by the nets, Granny nodded, all was well.

Kevin bothered no one, was no bother, liked a joke. True product of his parents, he gave a twinkling promise of well-intentioned mischief. Friendly, patient, laughing, he chose to give his time to Grandpa. Thick as thieves, they studied the form, and spoke in tongues. Kevin understood whistling Grandpa-ese. I didn't need to know Pa's words, his fluting tone was soft, spoke volumes.

Pa picked the winners, protégé placed the bets. Kevin built his future in that room.

Joe only stirred when Granny told him. Riddling the ashes, rattling the range. He performed the practised tasks with silvered ease. He was seemingly serene, open-necked, and neat-vested. When Granny commanded from another room, he sprayed polish in the air and hoovered slyly from his chair.

An automaton, he knew his own mind.
While behaving, he misbehaved;
while dutifully present, he was never there.

I was impressed, but his power came from the source he sought to outwit. Joe had inherited his mother's strength of will. In a circular way, she would always win.

Grandpa receded to the backgound like a cool colour while Grandma's fire roared and crackled. Seen shimmering through the heat-haze, a faithful and gentle ghost, he was more substantial than at first imagined. Someone had turned his sound down.

Someone had turned Joe's off.

Someone had blasted it loud enough to make his ears bleed.

He had a hatchet under his seat. He took it to his army photos.

Home

Once, Joe rose up through the water and broke the surface.

My concentration had faltered. Distracted by my drawing, I'd stopped sneaking glances at him. His knowing middle-distance stare had halted, and when I wasn't looking he took the pen from my hand. A watched pot never boils.

Joe spelt a coded message especially for me. I didn't understand it. Over the fireplace, its watchful eye angled downwards hanging from a chain, the mirror effortlessly unscrambled it.

Joe and I looked up into it and I saw us together. United, we shared the alchemy. Honoured, I was the sorcerer's apprentice and had stepped inside his cloak.

And You Read
Your Emily Dickinson

Jo Mazelis

Some time ago a man wrote a song about a woman reading some poems which had been written by another woman who lived her whole life in almost complete isolation. Then another man, whose name was Andy, played the record of the song to his girlfriend.

This was long ago in a first floor flat somewhere in the Uplands. There was an Indian bedspread hanging on the wall and another thrown over the settee. Dead joss sticks on the mantelpiece, white sweet-smelling ash on the tiles beneath. A candle in a bottle by the bed.

The girl, whose name was Marcie, didn't wear shoes for the whole of that summer. Maybe the year was 1976. Her feet grew hard and dirty, though her heart was as soft and sweet and delicate as an overripe strawberry.

One day, when they had been together for a week

or so, Andy had painted a delicate daisy chain around her ankle. It was done so exquisitely, so perfectly you would have thought it was real. She didn't want to wash after that. Just as sometimes after they had made love she didn't like to wash him away, but liked to feel his wetness seeping from her. Love, she thought, made all these things beautiful.

With autumn the rains came. At first the air grew hot and dry, and it seemed to hum with subdued energy. Then wind and lightning blasted themselves into being and the downpour began. The trees were stripped of their leaves overnight, it seemed.

The daisy chain had long faded from her ankle when he bought her a pair of black and white children's baseball boots from Woolworth's. They cost him seventy-five pence. For his twenty-third birthday she bought him Bob Dylan's just released 'Desire'.

They were locked in an oyster of time and all things were possible.

This is what it is to be young. It is as fleeting as a mayfly's summer, as intangible as the iridescent sheen on a dragonfly's wing.

In love, for that is what her condition was, she saw everything with an almost painfully acute clarity. The records he played for her seemed to speak directly from his soul to hers.

But then he ended it. And ended it in a crazy way. On the Monday he told her he loved her, on Tuesday he didn't ring her and on Wednesday he showed up with flowers.

'This may not make sense now,' he said, 'but one day

it will. I bought you these flowers as a sign of my love, but I also have something difficult that I want to say....'

Marcie had stood and watched Andy's face. Waited for his words. Expected him to say that he wanted to live with her or marry her or for her to have his baby.

'I think,' he said, 'I've been thinking. That is, I thought it would be best if we don't see each other anymore.'

It took her almost thirty years to get around to reading the Emily Dickinson poems mentioned in the song. Even though she'd always meant to.

This was when she found out about the poet's life: the years of seclusion in the upstairs room in Amherst. Little Emily, she thought, with her big mournful eyes and white muslin dresses lived the life of a ghost, her poems were the ink stains of a poltergeist, fragments left over from some twilight haunting.

She had bought a slim volume of Dickinson's collected poems from a charity shop and, prompted by a brief biography in the introduction, she had gone to the main library in the centre of town to find out more about the poet.

She was sitting on a row of chairs behind the stacks with Volume One of a Dickinson biography on her lap when she noticed a curious, but instantly recognizable noise. It was the sound of stifled sobs. Raggedy breathing, a wet choked sound, but yet so soft and feminine. Mournful cries smothered by propriety.

Because the Emily Dickinson biography was open on her lap, for one surreal moment she imagined that the sound of weeping came from the leaves of the book. She tried closing the book, by way of experiment, and the sounds did momentarily cease, but then they started again: little gasps of acute pain falling like a hesitant summer shower. She looked around for the source of the noise. On the other side of the library there was a row of four computers, which provided Internet access. All of the computers were occupied; four people sat with their backs to her, their shoulders hunched in that familiar and busy way. From where she was she could see the kind of things they were looking at on the screens, but she could not read anything. A bulky hulking woman in a loud floral dress was reading email from a hotmail account. A young man was looking at a picture of Marilyn Manson and his sweatshirt had the word Nirvana printed above a soulful picture of Kurt Cobain.

She watched and listened for the sounds and thought 'all things pass' but did not quite know where those words had come from. Perhaps it was a line from a song, perhaps a line printed on the inside of her skin; her maker's trademark like those on a doll or an item of clothing.

Dreaming, not quite concentrating, she heard the cries again and watched the young woman with the rippling auburn hair on the far end. This girl, hair aflame and skin as white and fragile as that on a store-bought mushroom, with her black boots and her black Lady Macbeth skirt and her black crocheted cardigan – a net for catching nightmares in – she had to be the weeper. Yet no quiver moved her body to the rhythm of the sobs. The girl was still and calm, except for when she too was finally driven to turn her head towards the noises of sorrow.

Then it was clear who the culprit was. The flesh beneath the floral print dress swelled and rippled like a breeze moving through a field of poppies.

'Oh,' the crying woman gasped, then breathed in sharply.

Then again, 'oh.'

The woman's head wobbled and faltered. It reminded Marcie of those Japanese dolls designed to warn of impending earthquakes. The woman's hair was cut very short and badly, emphasizing her solid, pink sausage neck.

Marcie wondered if someone would approach the woman to offer comfort, but no one did. Then she thought that perhaps she should do it if no one else – the librarians for example – would do it. She wondered what it was the woman had read on the screen that had upset her so. A lover's rejection? The news of a parent's death? Or that of an old friend or a much loved pet?

Marcie remembered how on the day so many years ago that Andy had finished with her, she had pretended to go to the bathroom, deliberately leaving behind her bag and coat with a plan to sneak from the house. She had not wanted to cry in front of him, and could not cope with his words about 'staying friends' and 'being mature'. How could she manage to be in his company and yet no longer reach for him, touch his hand, his thigh, his neck? Kiss him how and whenever she liked?

She'd tiptoed down the stairs, watching her feet as she went, willing them to silence. Tears were welling up in her eyes and she saw her feet as an abstracted pattern of black and white, black and white flashing over the red stair carpet. He'd clothed her feet in love. Even if it was only 75p's worth of Woolworth's love. Now he'd taken the love away and so she didn't want the shoes, didn't deserve them.

She sat on the bottom step and undid the laces. The boots had grown soft now and the new rubbery smell had worn off and the soles were getting thin in places.

She opened the front door and stepped out into the rain. There was a dustbin next to the porch and she lifted its silvery lid and dropped the boots in amongst the ashes and the potato peelings and the carcass of a chicken.

She set off for home. Down the hill she went, through the Uplands, a barefoot urchin with no coat, no money and no love. Tears poured down her cheeks and mixed with the rain. Her hair was plastered to her skull, her jeans grew dark and heavy and sodden. She sobbed. Her heart was breaking and yet an hour before she had been happy.

People passing stared at her. They watched from shop doorways and from under umbrellas and bus shelters. Heads turned to follow her progress as she passed pubs and cafes. No one went to her. No one offered succour. No one saw her pain as innocent or vulnerable or worth healing. She was instead freakishly mad, a wild girl on drugs. Dangerous.

She followed the road towards town, her thoughts now like a downpour, making dark puddles, mud holes of despair.

She was thinking of how there was nothing for her

now. That without his love the world was only rain and strangers.

But then from nowhere it seemed, there was a woman beside her, hurrying to keep pace.

'Excuse me. Excuse me,' was what the woman had said.

Marcie thought she was going to ask for directions, she stopped walking and looked at her.

The woman was middle-aged and wore a cream-coloured raincoat that flapped and blew in the wind. Under the raincoat she had on a pale blue blouse with a cameo brooch at her neck and a navy skirt. Her hair was short and styled in soft waves around her head, but very quickly it was being drenched and battered down by the rain.

'Are you alright?' the woman asked. 'Can I give you a lift somewhere?'

She gestured back up the road and Marcie saw a pale blue-green Morris Minor parked haphazardly under the trees, its headlights' silver beams illuminating the cascading raindrops.

Marcie hesitated, uncertain of what to do.

The woman waited and Marcie saw that she was getting soaked. Her hairstyle destroyed, her expensive clothes ruined. Soon the woman would look as bedraggled and pathetic as she did and then both of them would be outcasts.

The woman reached forward and touched Marcie's shoulder. She was both tentative and tender with that touch. It was the same as when one reaches for a stray dog, uncertain if the proffered hand will be licked or bitten.

'Come on,' said the woman with more confidence now, 'I can't leave you like this.'

And that was when Marcie had flung herself at the stranger and held her like you would hold your mother and she sobbed and sobbed and the woman made soothing noises, then led her to the car and tucked her into the passenger seat with the safety belt snugly around her like she was being tucked up in bed.

The woman's name was Sheila Berne. She had taken Marcie to her house, told her to shower, given her enormous warm towels and a dressing gown, then homemade soup and strong tea with whisky in.

They had sat together in the warm kitchen, rain still gusting against the windows and wind howling in the chimneys and Sheila had said: 'Now you tell me your troubles if you want to. Sometimes it helps. But if you don't want to that's fine too.'

Marcie told her, but as she arranged the words, it all seemed so paltry and pathetic – not the end of the world at all, not a reason for choosing not to live at all, but just a bad raw hiccup, that would be forgotten in years to come.

Later, with Marcie dressed in borrowed clothes, a summer frock from the Fifties, tennis shoes two sizes too big, and her wet clothes in a carrier bag, Sheila had dropped her home. As Marcie was getting out of the car, Sheila handed her a small slip of paper.

'There's my phone number and address. If you need me, call. You don't have to be alone.'

Marcie took the piece of paper and later that evening she tucked it in between the pages of a book. She had liked the idea that Sheila would always be there for her. Would open her door and heart to Marcie's despair if ever it got that bad again. She saved up the thought of Sheila like a last-chance talisman. Measured the degrees of her unhappiness by her need for Sheila. Three years went by and nothing was quite bad enough to warrant another visit. Then one day whilst tidying her belongings, Marcie came across the book which she believed held the slip of paper and fanned open the pages, but it wasn't there.

Thirty years later it was like a dream. She saw herself back then as a girl who was so vulnerable and gullible as to be downright idiotic. Life hardens the self as rough pavements harden the soles of the feet. Few things touched her now. Maybe that was why she was here today in the library seeking out Emily Dickinson and her hard nuggets of truth and pain and beauty.

Marcie thought about standing up and pretending to look at some books on the shelf a few feet away from the crying woman. From there she could read the email, but she knew this desire was more from curiosity than concern, and that stopped her.

She kept watching, willing someone in authority to go to the woman. Wasn't it part of the librarian's duty to help people? Wasn't it more proper for them to approach than for her, a complete stranger?

Then she thought: 'Well, if no one else will, then I must,' and just as she was about to lay the Emily Dickinson book down and rise from her chair in readiness to walk the ten or so paces, the woman suddenly closed the email page, stood up and hurried out.

What Marcie felt then was an incredible relief. She had planned to be good and kind, and would have done it, but now she was released.

She let out a breath and relaxed her shoulders and had the sensation that everyone else in the library was doing the same thing. The problem had picked herself up and left the building.

Marcie opened the book again and read one paragraph from the centre. It satisfied and tempted her just enough to make her borrow the heavyweight two-volume work and take it home.

She perused the rack of paperbacks for some time before leaving and decided to also borrow a murder mystery.

At the counter she handed over the plastic card with its barcode and considered mentioning the weeping woman to the librarian, but the man's brisk efficiency held her back. None of his business. None of her business. The computer system registered her presence, her loan for that day and she was done.

She left the library, negotiating the steps and the three young men who sat there smoking. She turned left in order to head for the bus, tucking the three books into her bag as she went. She still felt a faint nudge of guilt scratching at the inside of her head. She knew she should have gone to the woman sooner.

Then up ahead, stalled by a railing, she saw a hunched figure in a billowing tent-like dress, its splashing flowers garish amongst the city's grey backdrop of road and pavement and building.

Fifteen, maybe twenty minutes had passed, but the weeping woman had only got this far and still she wept.

Marcie slowed down, prepared herself for what she must do. This was her second chance. There was a debt to be paid and she could not baulk at it, no matter how futile it was, or how unwanted or silly.

She drew level with the woman.

'Excuse me,' she said, 'excuse me, but I noticed you were upset.'

The woman turned and Marcie saw her face for the first time. It was a swollen moon face, pink and bland with unfortunate bristles on the chin. The eyes were small and colourless and showed no life.

Marcie lifted her left hand and lightly batted the woman's well-padded shoulder with the flat of her palm. She sensed the swell of flesh, hot and damp beneath the thin cotton dress. She could not quite bring herself to rest her hand there.

'Is there anything I can do? Would it help to talk?'

The woman looked away. Closed herself off again in her sorrow.

Marcie persisted, 'Are you sure?'

'No,' the woman murmured, 'no.'

'Well,' said Marcie, as she gave the shoulder one last clumsy pat, 'I'll leave you then.'

And then Marcie walked away without a backward glance; her account still partially in arrears.

Biographies

Isabel Adonis

Isabel Adonis is a writer, artist, mother of four children whom she home educated, a regular columnist of *Diverse Minds*, a black mental health magazine, and sits on their National Advisory Panel. She is the co-founder of The Meeting Pool which was set up as a forum for culture and identity and has recently published a new multicultural journal called *Timbuktu*. Isabel lives with her partner, Bob, in north Wales: she has two allotments, loves riding her bike, salsa dance classes and swimming in the sea.

Glenda Beagan

Glenda Beagan has published two collections of short stories, *The Medlar Tree* and *Changes and Dreams* (both Seren), and a collection of poems, *Vixen* (Honno). Her work has appeared in many anthologies, including *The New Penguin Book of Welsh Short Stories*, *The Green Bridge* and *Magpies*. Apart from time spent studying as a mature student at Aberystwyth, where she was awarded First Class Honours in English, and at Lancaster, where she gained an MA in Creative Writing, she has lived all her life in Rhuddlan.

Leonora Brito

Leonora Brito was born in Cardiff. She won the Rhys Davies Short Story Competition in 1991. Her first collection, *Dat's Love*, was published in 1995; her new collection, *Chequered Histories*, in 2005.

Alexandra Claire
Alexandra Claire was born and brought up in and around Cardiff. She trained at London Contemporary Dance School before working as a dancer and choreographer throughout Europe. She now works in the electricity industry and lives in Cardiff with her four-year-old daughter.

Lewis Davies
Lewis Davies was born in Penrhiwtyn in 1967. He has won a number of awards for his writing.

Geoff Dunn
Geoff Dunn was born and brought up in Milford Haven but spent many years teaching languages in the Midlands. He now lives in Ciliau Aeron. His story, *Only On A Sunday Morning*, won first prize in the Cardigan/Aberteifi Purple Dragon Short Story Competition.

Miranda Evans
Miranda Evans was born in Cardigan in 1967 and brought up in Pembrokeshire. She has a degree in Fine Art, and works as a media production technician. She lives with her husband near Carmarthen. This is the first story she has written.

Thomas Fourgs
Thomas Fourgs lives in Cardiff. *Spookfish* – a collection of short stories – is published by Parthian.

Jon Gower
Jon Gower is the arts and media correspondent for BBC Wales. His books include the short story collection *Big Fish*; a travel book about Chesapeake Bay called *An Island Called Smith*; a volume of local history called *A Long Mile*; and he has edited *Homeland*, *I Know Another Way*, and *A Year in a Small Country*. He is currently working on a biography of actor Steve Buscemi.

Niall Griffiths
Niall Griffiths was born in Liverpool in 1966 and has lived in mid-Wales for well over a decade. He has published five novels and is working on a sixth – *Runt*. *Stump* won the Welsh Book of the Year award and *Kelly + Victor* is to be filmed. In addition, Niall has had short pieces (both fiction and non-fiction) published all over the place, has read his work in many countries, and has been translated into several languages.

Tristan Hughes
Tristan Hughes was born in Atikokan, Canada. He was educated at Ysgol David Hughes, Menai Bridge, and the universities of York and Edinburgh, and at King's College, Cambridge. In 2002 he won the Rhys Davies Award and *The Tower*, his first book, was published in 2003. He is currently at work on a second novel, *The Strange Journeying Of Johnny Ifor Jones*, to be published in 2005.

Cynan Jones

Cynan Jones' story is from his first book *After the Factory*.

Huw Lawrence

Huw Lawrence has had articles, stories and poems published in *The Critical Quarterly*, *New Welsh Review*, *Planet*, *Poetry Wales*, *The Inheritor's House*, and other magazines. He was a prizewinner in the 1999 Rhys Davies Competition. He lives in Aberystwyth where he is working on a novel.

Jo Mazelis

Jo Mazelis's first book, *Diving Girls*, was short-listed for Welsh Book of the Year and Commonwealth Best First Book. She has been a prizewinner in the Rhys Davies Short Story Competition three times. Her stories and poetry have appeared in *New Welsh Review*, *Poetry Wales*, *Big Issue*, *Citizen 32*, and *nth position*, as well as being broadcast by Radio Four. Her second collection of stories, *Circle Games*, is published by Parthian.

Siân Preece

Siân Preece was born in Wales, and lived in Canada and France for five years before moving to Aberdeen. Her first story collection, *From the Life*, was published in 2000 by Polygon. She writes stories and drama for Radio Four, and contributes to the *Sunday Herald* newspaper. She has appeared in several anthologies, including *Mama's Baby (Papa's Maybe)* (Parthian) and *Scottish Girls About Town* (Simon and Schuster). She recently completed a novel.

lloyd robson

lloyd robson is a writer, workshop tutor and gun-for-hire text operative. As a writer, he is author of *letter from sissi*, *cardiff cut* and *bbboing!* As a visual artist, he produced the *sense of city road* project. His work is widely published and has been translated into several languages.

Rhian Saadat

Rhian lives and works in Paris. Her collection of poetry, *Window Dressing for Hermes*, is published by Parthian.

Brian Smith

Brian Smith was born in the north-west of England and has lived and worked in Wales for over thirty years. He is on the editorial board of *Roundyhouse* poetry magazine and has published short stories, picture books and poems in the UK and abroad.

Rachel Trezise

Rachel Trezise is author of *In And Out of the Goldfish Bowl*, which won the Orange Futures Award in 2002.